Here Comes
to Light You

Maggie Prince grew up in Lancaster and now
lives in Hertfordshire where she combines writing
with teaching. Her earlier books for Orion were
Memoirs of a Dangerous Alien, which won the 1995
WH Smith's Mind-Boggling Books Award, and its
sequel, *Pulling the Plug on the Universe*. She has also
written some for younger readers, *Dragon in the
Drainpipe*, *Dragon in the Family*, *The Glory Hole*,
Rachel on the Run and *Wishing Powder* published
by Hodder Headline, and *Witch Hill* published by
Blackie.

Here comes a candle to light you to bed
And here comes a chopper to chop off your head

Anon. From 'Oranges and Lemons', a nursery rhyme and children's dancing game, of which an earlier version, 'Oringes and Lemons', appears as a square-for-eight dance in Playford's *Dancing Master* of 1665.

Here Comes a Candle to Light You to Bed

MAGGIE PRINCE

A Dolphin
Paperback

Acknowledgments

My warmest thanks go to my researchers, Dan Groenewald and Deb Groenewald, who uncovered a lot of fascinating and horrifying information, and to the staff of various libraries, particularly Berkhamsted Public Library and Tower Hamlets Local History Library and Archive.

Published as a
Dolphin Paperback in 1997

First published in Great Britain in 1996
by Orion Children's Books
a division of the Orion Publishing Group Ltd
Orion House, 5 Upper St Martin's Lane
London WC2H 9EA

A catalogue record for this book
is available from the British Library

Typeset at The Spartan Press Ltd,
Lymington, Hants

Printed in Great Britain by
Clays Ltd, St Ives plc

ISBN 1 85881 384 0

One

*T*HERE IS SOMETHING HORRIBLE IN JONAH'S room. I know it. Yet nobody else seems to notice.

Oh, not just his old socks and Megadeth tapes, though those are certainly horrible enough. No, I mean something I don't understand. Something frightening.

All I've had is a glimpse, and I have to admit that I was very tired at the time. I know it's possible to think you see strange things when you're very tired, and I was quite simply exhausted. Exams and a house move all at the same time are not a good combination.

As for the parent thing — well, what can I say?

I go downstairs. These are still unfamiliar stairs, wooden, worn into a smooth hollow in the middle of each tread, turning sharply to the left half way down. You can sit in the top half and hear what is going on downstairs and not be seen. This time, though, the stairs creak.

'Emily?' It is Mum's voice. 'Emily? Do you want a cup of tea? Roger is here.'

I almost turn and go back up. Really, this is too much. The fat know-all from next door who is always trying to impress Mum just can't seem to keep away. Still, the only way to get to the teapot and by implication the chocolate cake tin is to go down. Mum's guilt trip since she and Dad split up five months ago does have some advantages. A constant supply of home-made chocolate cake is one of them.

'Do sit down, Roger,' Mum is saying as I go into the living room. He places his fat bottom delicately into the best chair. Its castors squeak on the stone floor, making a sound as if he had farted. I look at him intently then smile sympathetically to indicate that I understand small human failings. Roger reddens.

This is quite the smallest house I have ever lived in. On the other side of the living room door is the pavement. The ceiling with its head-stunning beams is low and the walls sometimes feel as is they are crowding in on me, advancing towards me like nightmare walls in a James Bond torture chamber. All we need is the rising water to complete a real horror scenario. Instead we have this drip from next door.

'Emily,' he gushes. 'And how's my favourite schoolgirl today?' I wrinkle my brow in a look of deliberate incomprehension and glance behind me as if looking for his favourite schoolgirl. Mum scowls at me. Tough. If she wants to encourage this silly man when she had a perfectly adequate husband who was funny and clever and *really* knew things, then she must take the consequences.

'How did your exams go?' Roger continues, addressing me but looking at Mum with vomit-inducing adoration. He stretches his legs out, making himself at home. Home, that's a joke. We moved here eight weeks ago after our real home was finally sold at the end of the summer term.

I do not answer him. I get away with my rudeness only because Jonah comes in, treading mud from his Doc Martens all over the flagstones.

'Jonah!' snaps Mum. 'Boots!'

I go into the kitchen to fetch the chocolate cake tin.

Later, when we are both back upstairs doing our homework, I call out through my open bedroom door, 'Jonah?'

'Hm?' It sounds as if he is concentrating but I don't care. I go into his room which is across the uneven landing from mine. Mum gave us the best rooms. It was the guilt thing again. She sleeps in a room that is scarcely more than a cupboard, but she says she doesn't mind so long as she has privacy and her own space. Private it may be, but space it is not.

I have to brace myself to go into Jonah's room. I have felt this reluctance from the beginning. I thought it was simply that the sun does not shine so directly in here. I chose the other of the two large bedrooms even though this one is slightly bigger and looks down the hill towards the park.

Once over the threshold I pause and look around. There is always the possibility of course that I am going mad. People do. It isn't unheard of. Mad Emily of Hound Hill. I could trail the streets giggling insanely and spitting and breaking windows and everyone would feel sorry for me. Yes, *at least* then everyone would feel sorry for me. They don't now. At sixteen my life is in ruins but they still expect me to take exams and write essays and understand equations.

Jonah's room is a mess. It is always a mess. It was the same at the old house, the one we shared with Dad. Tapes, underwear, books, ancient half-drunk cups of coffee, one with a bluish crusty layer on top, litter the floor. I take another step in and an empty crisp packet rustles under my foot. A tree's branches rustle outside the window. Suddenly I can go no further.

'What is it?' Jonah is slumped on his beanbag by the radiator. He doesn't look up from what he is reading.

'Jonah, your room . . .'

Now he looks up. 'Oh don't you start. It's bad enough with Mum going on about my room.'

'No, no . . .' I speak hurriedly to reassure him. 'It's

just . . . I mean . . . this may sound stupid but have you ever seen anything odd in your room, Jonah?'

Now he's really looking at me, and suddenly I am afraid, because he is not denying it. He is not saying what do you mean. He is putting down his book.

'No,' he says.

I exhale slowly and glance round me once again, towards the corners, along the line of the door towards the hinge, over to where the long curtains sway in a breeze from the window. On the far wall my own face looks back at me from Jonah's mirror, a rather pink face with pale hair, distorted because the mirror was cracked in the move.

Forcing myself, I take another step forward and sit on a packing box which has still not been emptied, even though it is so many weeks since we moved.

'What do you mean?' Jonah asks me. '*Anything odd.*'

I shake my head. 'Nothing.' I look at Jonah. It is a warm autumn day but suddenly I see that gooseflesh is standing up all along his arms below his t-shirt sleeves. He rubs at them, below the elbow.

I stand up and back towards the door. I think of the stair treads, the hollowed out stair treads, and I know that there is a hollow in the atmosphere of this room that is the same, something worn away and waiting to be filled. And in that moment there is nothing, absolutely nothing, that would make me stay in Jonah's room.

Two

'ACTUALLY, ROGER, I PROBABLY DID RATHER badly in my exams.' I am standing on the pavement next morning waiting for Jonah, and I have decided belatedly to answer our neighbour's question. He is vigorously cleaning the outsides of his windows, and it is barely eight thirty. It does occur to me to wonder why I so much dislike this obviously hard-working and friendly man.

'Oh, I'm so sorry, my dear. Well, better luck next time. I went to that school, you know, St Wolfstan's, when I was a lad. It seems to be a new thing they've brought in, these autumn exams. Oh well never mind. You'll get used to it. I expect it was hard for you to concentrate, under the circumstances.'

I glare at him. How dare he mention our circumstances? But he is gazing away down the hill towards the park and the church spire beyond. A cool wind is blowing down the hill. I hug my thick duffle coat around me. Roger gets down from his stepladder. I am taller than he is. I am like Dad and Jonah, tall and thin. Mum is the short one. Maybe she and Roger deserve each other.

'Hurry up, Jonah!' I yell back into the house, then look again at our neighbour who to my surprise is staring at his surroundings with an expression of extreme unease.

'This wasn't always called Hound Hill, you know,' he says in an odd tone. 'A hundred years ago it was called Beggarsgate. Its name was changed last century when it was being gentrified by the Victorians.'

I look at him, reluctantly interested. He is wringing out what looks like a piece of old vest in his bucket of soapy water.

'Really?' I can see Jonah struggling into his boots now, just inside the doorway.

Roger nods. 'Oh yes. A lot of places like this, towards the edges of London, had their street names changed to something more salubrious. I suppose the Victorians preferred the idea of the hunt streaming down the hill to the thought of beggars streaming down it.'

Jonah emerges. We say goodbye to Roger and cut through the narrow alley between his house and ours. Mum's cupboard bedroom is like a bridge over the alley, with a small window looking out on to the street. Behind the houses the alley opens out into a flagstoned courtyard with the backs of the houses in the next street at the far side. There is a single tree in the middle of the courtyard. It is an oak, and appears to be very ancient. It is not tall, but gnarled and twisted, deprived of light like a caged animal, its bark curling off in places. A further alley takes us through to the main road and the hill down towards school.

St Wolfstan's Mixed Comprehensive must, I'm sure, have some redeeming characteristics. It's just that I can't think of them. Jonah and I pleaded and begged to be allowed to continue at our old schools. We offered bribes in the form of promises to wash up for all eternity. We offered to work in the evenings and at weekends to help pay the fees. We said we wouldn't mind the two hour trek across town to get to and from our schools. I regret every moment I grumbled about school in the past. It seems very precious now.

It was all useless. Mum and Dad explained that the cost of living separately was so much more than the cost of living together, that there was no question of continuing private education. The fees had been difficult to manage at the best of times. We were lucky, Mum told us, to be able to live in a house of such character as 103 Beggarsgate.

I stop in my tracks. Why did I say that? Think it, not say it, though it feels as if I said it. 103 Hound Hill, she said. Of course she did. She has no inkling of its ever having been called Beggarsgate. Yet to me, in my mind, it has become Beggarsgate.

'Emily?' Jonah has stopped too and is staring at me. 'What's the matter?'

I shake my head. I feel near to tears. 'I'm not going to school, Jonah,' I say. I open my bag, take out my peanut butter and marmalade sandwiches and start eating them. 'I know I've failed all my exams. I'm just not going there, to be humiliated.'

Jonah is in the class below me. There is just a year between us. His class did not have this extra lot of exams, supposedly designed to prepare us for the big ones in the summer.

'What, you're going to play truant?' He looks shocked and impressed, then glances suddenly beyond me.

'Good morning Jonah, Emily,' says a voice. I turn. It is Miss Patel, our sociology teacher. I have only had her for one lesson as she has been away in India visiting her sick mother. 'You two had better hurry up or you'll be late. I don't know what's got into everybody this morning.' She glances round at other hurrying figures clutching books and school bags. 'I'm just as bad too, this morning. I don't know where the time has gone to.' She strides past us but I call out to her.

'Miss Patel! I'm not going to school today.'

She stops and turns to stare at me.

'What, Emily? Are you ill?'

I shake my head, wishing I had just sneaked off instead. 'No. But I know I've failed all my exams. I don't want to go in. I'm just not going.' I can hear my voice rising. Suddenly I really don't care. I couldn't care less what she says, and it is liberating.

Miss Patel faces me, frowning, and adjusts her sari. Out of the corner of my eye I can see Jonah fidgeting from one foot to the other and glancing at his watch.

'Go on,' I say to him. 'Don't wait. I'll see you tonight.'

He looks reluctant, then rummages in his school bag — ours are formal leather satchels, out of place and embarrassing in this new educational situation of canvas rucksacks and nylon sports bags — and produces a squashed bar of chocolate. 'Here.' He thrusts it at me, then hurries off.

Miss Patel is staring at me with her head on one side.

'We all do badly in exams sometimes, Emily, and it has to be faced just like anything else.'

'Oh, so I have done badly.'

'Well I can only speak for sociology, but yes. Now let's have no more of this nonsense. It's not the end of the world, you know.'

I turn and start walking, away from her, across the broad pavement, towards the next alley between the houses.

'Emily!' Miss Patel hurries after me. Reluctantly I stop, and glare at her. She pauses instead of speaking. Finally she says, 'I can't force you to go to school, but you will have to eventually, you know. However I can see that you are distraught just now. I hope you are not sickening for something. Go home then and I'll call in with your results later on, this evening probably. I just live a little way up Hound Hill from you.' She nods and walks on.

Jonah has gone now. A few other late stragglers are rushing down the hill, bags flapping. I ignore them, although I know some of them, and veer off, back through this other alley which comes out near the park and the church. Go home, she said, but I can never go home again, and I would rather go almost anywhere than back to the house on Hound Hill.

It is very quiet in the alley and on the bottom part of Hound Hill where it levels out near the park. There is hardly anyone about. It is as if school has sucked all human life off the streets and into its greedy jaws. At least I am not easily identifiable as a truant, because at this school we do not wear uniforms.

I enter the park, touching my hand briefly to the flaking green-painted spikes of the wrought iron gates. They feel cold despite the sunshine.

There are curving paths through flowering shrubberies here, and small woods of beech, sycamore and oak on low hills, burning with the colours of autumn. It has open spaces and flowerbeds. It has a small lake.

I walk round the lake to the copse of beech trees at the far side. The ground beneath them is bare and earthy. It smells damp and raw. Skeletal traces of last year's leaves lie among tree roots, but this year's leaves have not fallen yet. A clump of large black toadstools clusters by this far boundary wall and railing. There is something else here too, a rectangular stone of some sort, half set into the ground almost against the boundary wall, leaning lopsidedly. I cross over to it and crouch down.

It has obviously been looked after. There is a little trough of neat, cleared earth around it, and a tiny blackened wire fence. There is lettering engraved into the stone but it is so worn that I cannot decipher the words. Suddenly I notice a small wooden plaque at the back of the fencing, against the boundary wall itself. This is easier to read. I peer more closely.

This historical monument is under
the protection of Hound Hill
Museum and Local History Society.

Now I must know what is engraved on the stone. There appear to be some numbers at the beginning of the inscription. I trace them with my fingers. Unlike the wrought iron earlier, they feel warm. Some of them I can make out, a six, then further down, a nought or an o.

I take my can of Coke from my school bag, open it and dip my handkerchief into it, feeding a corner further and further into the hole made by the ring-pull. Then I wipe the wet material across the top of the time-blurred lettering, reminded for some reason of Roger and his window cleaning. At once some of the letters stand out, dusty and dun coloured against the dark wetness. There is a one before the six, then further down a t and an e together followed by 'memorye of . . .' This is clearly very old, to judge by the antiquated spelling. Most of the words are simply too eroded to read, but the last word, after some concentration, seems to be 'soules'.

I am puzzled, but now my knees are uncomfortable so I stand up. There is a massive beech tree behind me whose trunk curves at the bottom into what is almost a horizontal seat, before disappearing into the earth. I sit down on it. I find that I have a headache and feel slightly sick. Perhaps I am ill after all. Perhaps I do have a legitimate reason for being off school. This is rather comforting.

I lean back against the rough bark and look at where the trunk slopes away into the ground beyond my feet.

There are a few tufts of grass here where the wood curls into contorted shapes and disappears from sight. A small bird, a wren, appears, hopping among the roots, through the grass. It does not seem to notice me.

This is a peaceful place, but I do not feel peaceful. I feel tense and depressed. Suddenly the wren gives a startled chirrup and shoots off into the branches of the beech tree. I look round to see what has frightened it, but I can see nothing. As I stand up, something brushes against my leg and I gasp with shock, but then I see that it is only a small leafy twig growing out of the base of the trunk.

I look over at the stone. The wetness is drying now. The inscription is fading. Soon it will be gone. Later I will ask someone what it means. Perhaps I will ask Miss Patel when she brings my disastrous exam results round this evening.

Place.

Three

*I*N THE END THERE IS NOWHERE ELSE TO GO BUT back to the house. As I walk with slow steps out of the park I wonder about the Hound Hill Museum, mentioned on the plaque. I had never heard of it before. It must be further up the hill from where we live.

I feel nervous as I approach our front door. There seems to be no one about but I feel as if I am being watched. Mum *should* have gone to work. It ought to be all right. The day is getting warmer. Birds are singing somewhere near. I feel a surge of unexpected cheerfulness.

There is no sign of Roger as I put my key in the lock, for which I am thankful. Not that I couldn't deal with him. It's none of his business why I'm not at school. I suddenly realise what I don't like about Roger. It's his attitude that he knows what's right for other people better than they do themselves, a sort of unspoken claim to extra common sense.

I feel abruptly that it's actually all right to dislike Roger, that I'm not being unreasonable or un-neighbourly, that it's even fine to hate him if I want to. I'm me; I can think and feel as I like. The sun comes out very brightly just then and shines right down the street, and I experience another moment like the one in which I realised I didn't care what Miss Patel thought. It's as if little pieces of armour plating are flaking away. I feel exposed and vulnerable, but open and excited too.

I have a moment of misgiving as I push the door open. What if Mum has a morning off from her temporary job at Le Plastique jewellery shop, or a late start today?

The house feels empty. There is complete silence through the rooms. I sidle across the living room and into the kitchen, gradually relaxing. I put the kettle on and make instant coffee, very strong, with four teaspoons of sugar. I walk to the back door which leads out into a dank, narrow alley with a high wall. This is an even smaller alley than the one between the houses, which it leads down to. It is cobblestoned and the cobblestones are green with tuffets of moss between them. Some people leave their dustbins out in this cramped place, blocking it completely. It is dark and smelly and the sky seems a long way off above the high grey wall.

I stand in the open doorway, despairing that I have to live here. As I slam the door shut again the old cat flap, installed by the previous owners, swings and creaks. I kick it, feeling near to tears again. We had a cat where we used to live with Dad. *Have* a cat, not had. Her name is Andromeda. Dad has kept her because she was his cat to start with. She is extremely old as cats go, eighteen and a half, and at the end of each visit to Dad's new flat I wonder if I will ever see her again.

Furious and sad, I feel a great desire to break something. I understand about people who vandalise telephone boxes. The problem is, if I vandalise the kitchen, I will have to clear up the mess. I thump one of the doors of the incredibly old-fashioned kitchen range, and hurt my hand.

This kitchen range really has to be seen to be believed. It is made of black iron with a fireplace in the middle and a mantelpiece over the top. On either side of the fireplace are two little ovens with heavy iron doors. 'Bread ovens,' the previous owner explained when he was showing us round. He was warming his slippers in one of them. There is a brown-tiled hearth with a black iron fender round it. I kick the fender and it makes a clanging noise. The sound echoes through the house. I'm glad, because the house has been starting to feel a little bit too quiet.

I switch the television on in the living room, but as I do, there is another sound. It is indistinguishable because of the sudden blare of noise from the television set. Abruptly I switch off again and stand very still, listening. The echo from the fender has died away. What was it? What did I hear at the very moment of pressing the switch? As far as I can recapture it, it seemed like a sort of scutter.

I'm not afraid of mice. When Roger told us he had mice I said smoothly, 'How absolutely lovely. They're dear little things, aren't they,' because he so obviously thought they were disgusting. Now, though, I feel that I would prefer not to be alone with one, particularly when I am not sure where it is and from which direction it might dash to surprise me.

I continue to stand and wait. The house is completely silent. Sounds come in from outside, the hissing of a lorry's air brakes on the hill, half-hearted birdsong from the direction of the courtyard at the back, an aeroplane, the far siren of some emergency vehicle, someone whistling 'Greensleeves'.

At last I give up. The scutter, too, was probably a sound from outside, or maybe one of Roger's mice just passing through. I decide against switching the television back on and instead I go upstairs to my bedroom.

The door to Jonah's room is open. I hurry by, deciding I will simply not start thinking about it.

Suddenly I realise what I could do today, this day out

of time when nobody knows where I am. I could take the Tube across London to my old school. I could visit my old friends, see my old classroom and for a while pretend that everything is all right. This seems an absolute brainwave.

I change into a more comfortable pair of jeans and a knee-length blue jumper and tip out my allowance box. Mum still calls our pathetic weekly handout an 'allowance', even though it is only a quarter of what it used to be. It's nice to see she hasn't entirely lost her sense of humour.

I count up. There is enough. I can travel across London and back, and buy lunch for myself and Samantha too. I feel elated. It will be wonderful to see my best friend again. We have been together since we both started at the school. She is a boarder, a very brainy girl from Yorkshire. We were always giggling together through lessons, so quite how she managed to get the spectacular exam results she did is a mystery. Now I can only see her occasionally at weekends, and it is not the same.

The grandfather clock is striking ten downstairs in the living room. It is time to go. I have to get past Jonah's room again. I stuff my money into my back jeans pocket, delaying the moment of walking out of my room. What, I ask myself, if Jonah's door were now *shut* instead of open, when I cross the landing? I rub my arms briskly and manage a little laugh. It really doesn't do to start thinking like this when you're alone in the house.

Of course, all of it could simply be mice. There might just be mice in Jonah's room. How silly it would be if I had allowed an innocent little mouse to give me this feeling of dread. I might unconsciously have noticed a faint and unfamiliar smell, perhaps the tiniest of sounds behind the skirting board, things like that.

I stop at my bedroom door and try to remember exactly what it was I saw, that time. It was a movement, by the wall. Well, not so much *by* the wall as *in* the wall. A shimmer, a shift of perspective, then nothing, just plain old wall again. Now Jonah's big chest of drawers is up against that wall, hiding it, and he sleeps unknowingly shut in his room with the thing trapped behind chaotic swathes of socks and boxer shorts.

This is crazy. Should I warn him? What could I say? We have to go on living here, that has been made very clear. All I would achieve would be to make Jonah as frightened as I am, and despite the gooseflesh on his arms yesterday, he does not appear actually to be afraid of being in his room.

I force myself out on to the landing. My headache and sick feeling are coming back. This is ridiculous. I must think about other things, the park, the stone, the sunshine.

Of course the door to Jonah's room is not shut. It is exactly as it was when I last passed it a few minutes ago. I laugh to myself and start to go downstairs, keeping an eye on the open doorway nevertheless, over my shoulder. Once I have turned the bend of the stairs the front door is just across the living room. If necessary I could make a dash and be out of there in seconds. I glance back one last time. Then I remember that I have left the back door in the kitchen unlocked.

I take several deep breaths. This is just silly. Wait till I tell Samantha all about it. The thought gives me strength. I stand up straight with my shoulders back and march loudly down the last few steps of the wooden staircase, thump thump thump. I whistle a few bars of 'Greensleeves', the tune I heard coming from outside earlier. I smile as I remember what Great Grandmother Strachan says if ever I dare to whistle in her presence. 'A whistling woman and a crowing hen / Will bring the Devil from his den.'

I saunter across the living room, still whistling, and into the kitchen, my hand stretched out to turn the key in the back door lock. Half way across the rough stone floor I look up at the little window over the sink. Someone is looking in.

Four

FOR A MOMENT THE SHOCK IS SO INTENSE THAT I think I might just pass out. My heart gives a terrible thud and my breath goes in sharply and doesn't come out again.

The face looks as if it has been there for a while. It is completely unmoving. We stand there, just staring at each other, for several moments.

Then I step forward and say loudly, 'What do you want?' By now I am realising that this might be the milkman or window cleaner or dustman on perfectly legitimate business. The face does not smile or reply. It is male, with long dark hair tied back. He is maybe a couple of years older than me.

Then he taps at the window and raises his eyebrows. I feel I have no option but to step forward and open the door. It is very unusual for people to come round the back, considering how difficult it is to get there. Nevertheless, if he were a mad axeman he would probably have barged through the door by now rather than waiting politely, so I turn the handle and tug at the door. For a moment it will not open, which is odd, because usually it is loose and lets a draught in. I wrench at it and finally it flies open almost knocking me backwards. The young man turns from the window to face me. He half smiles, but I do not.

'Yes?' My voice sounds hostile and suspicious as I lean

out slightly to look at him. It is dim in the alley but I can see that he is dressed in a strange and rather hippyish coat and high, baggy boots. He speaks, and it immediately becomes obvious that he is a foreigner. I catch a couple of words, but his English is so bad and so heavily accented that I cannot understand him.

'I'm sorry. I'm afraid I can't . . .'

He sighs and bends down and swishes his hand along at boot level — his boots are amazing — and says 'Cat?'

'Cat? What about a cat?' I listen carefully. He does seem to be harmless, if a bit peculiar.

'I seek my cat.'

'Ah!' I laugh triumphantly. 'You've lost your cat! Is that it?'

He is clearly having equal difficulty in understanding me, but now he nods doubtfully.

'Oh, I'm sorry.' I shake my head. 'I haven't seen a cat round here. What does it look like?' I make different shapes and sizes with my hands so that he knows what I mean. He grins, with a gleam in his eye, and speaks again, and I find I am getting used to his garbled speech, and understanding more.

'A small cat, black, a thin kitten with a bent tail.'

'Ahh,' I say soppily. 'How sweet. I'll look out for it.'

I become aware of the sound of a handbell tolling in the street at the front of the house, the sort of bell that rag-and-bone men still use in some areas as they drive slowly round the streets. It is being rung irregularly, as if by someone very tired indeed. The expression hardens on the face of the stranger. I feel a dark sense of oppression myself suddenly, as he looks beyond me, almost through me. The sound of the bell grows nearer, passes, then starts to fade.

The young man looks into my face. Even in the uncertain light of the narrow passage I can see that his eyes are brown, like toffee. The moment stretches out.

'I can see into the future,' he says abruptly.

I feel a pang of regret. Oh dear, a nutcase, what a pity.

'You'd better give me your phone number or address,' I say, 'in case I do see your cat.'

He nods and gives a small bow. 'I am obliged. I live at 103 Beggarsgate, in the lodgings over the bakehouse.' Then before I can express surprise, or even take it in properly, he is gone, striding fast into the darkness of the alley, out of sight without seeming to have any difficulty in walking over the slime and moss, or in squeezing past the graceless wheelie bins.

By lunchtime I am on the other side of London walking through the tall stone gates of my old school. I am still unnerved by my encounter with the weird boy in the alley, obviously some sort of history freak judging by his use of the street's old name. He was lucky I didn't realise sooner how crazy he was or I wouldn't have spoken to him at all. 103 Beggarsgate indeed. What sort of stupid game was he trying to play?

I stroll off across the school lawn, trying to remember my old timetable and work out where Samantha will be at eleven forty-five on a Monday.

I find her in the bright study room which she shares with two other seniors. She is practising her elocution. The door is half open. 'Bakam,' I hear her say. 'Ba*kum*, bu*kam* . . .'

'Sam?'

'Emily!' she shrieks, reverting to her normal voice. 'Em! Hey! I can't believe it!'

'What *are* you doing?' I ask, indicating what looks like a list of words written phonetically, in the form of how they sound.

'Oh . . .' She rolls her eyes. 'I'm learning to speak posh, duckie. Have you noticed how they say "become" down here? Well of course you have. You're one of them. Anyway, it's partly Mrs Protheroe's elocution lessons and partly my ever-continuing efforts to try and fit in here.' She slams the book shut, muttering 'Ba*kam*' under her breath. 'How are you doing? What are you doing here? Shouldn't you be in school?'

I look round longingly. *This* is school. Here there is space, space for everyone. There are textbooks for everyone too, no sharing. I decide, since it's Samantha, that I can treat myself to a good cry.

She hugs me and says, 'Hey Em, is it really bad?'

So I tell her about my own totally unsuccessful efforts to fit in at my new school, about not understanding the work because the courses are different, about doing badly in the exams, about missing my friends and Dad and Andromeda. I tell her that I hate the house and hate Roger and that I am afraid he is after Mum, which is almost too revolting to articulate.

Then, when I have told her all this, and she has made me a cup of tea with the kettle and teabags she and her friends keep in the corner for when they are studying, I tell her about Jonah's room. She stares at me round-eyed and runs both her hands up through her red hair so that it stands on end.

'What . . . you mean you think the house is haunted?'

I shrug miserably.

'I don't know. Maybe it's just me. Maybe I'm haunted. When I'm back here I can hardly believe that place exists. The whole situation is like something out of a nightmare or a horror story.'

Just then one of the girls with whom she shares the room comes in, Rose, the resident pot smoker.

'Sammikins, are you ready to come to lunch?' trills

— 21 —

Rose. 'The boys are waiting.' When she sees me she screams and throws her arms in the air. She is re-markably un-laid-back for someone who is permanently stoned.

When I have told her why I am here and we have talked for a few more moments Rose explains that the three of them are going out for lunch with three boys from one of the bands which are playing for tonight's school dance. I feel insane with jealousy. This should have been me.

'Can you come to lunch too?' asks Samantha dutifully. Good Sam, nice Sam, brought up to be polite.

I shake my head. 'No. No, thanks. I have to get back.'

'Oh, don't go back so soon,' Rose protests. 'We've hardly talked. Stay here and wait for us, and come to the dance this evening. It's going to be great. We've got three really deadly bands. Sammy and I organised it all. We found them ourselves.'

'Leaving no turn unstoned,' Samantha grins. They double up with laughter and I realise that these two now talk in the same inter-active way that Samantha and I used to, interrupting each other and providing the cues for each other's jokes. I know now that I no longer fit in here. I have gone from this place with steps that cannot be retraced. I have gone to another place where I also don't fit in. There seems to be nowhere on earth where I can exist and be myself in peace. I feel shut in by my misery, enclosed and imprisoned, with no way of stretching out a hand to the real world outside.

Five

*I*GO HOME SLOWLY, NOT BOTHERING WITH LUNCH. Food seems completely unappealing. I get off the Tube two stops early and walk and get lost and eventually find my way home by recognising the church spire near the park and following it like a beacon. I wonder again about the stone and the wooden plaque as I pass the park gates and start off up Hound Hill.

Jonah is home already. He is sitting in a corner of the living room smoking Gauloises and reading the encyclopaedia.

'Hi Jonah. How was school?' I flop down in a chair. I feel dusty and exhausted.

'Hi. Oh, same as usual. Patel said to tell you she'll be here at eight. There's tea in the pot.' He is keeping his place in the book with his finger, and he goes back to it immediately. I had forgotten about Miss Patel. This really feels like the last straw. I go and pour myself some tea then come back and try to get Jonah's attention.

'There was a peculiar boy here this morning. He was looking for his cat. Have you seen a small black cat with a bent tail?'

Jonah looks at me.

'Yes.' He lets the book drop shut. 'You know ... that's so bizarre ... I wasn't sure if it was a dream or not.' He shakes his head. 'You know when you get up in the night to go to the loo and you're hardly awake so it's a bit like sleepwalking?'

I nod. Our bathroom and lavatory are downstairs next to the kitchen in this house, so I avoid middle of the night trips to them, but I know from before, when I could wander the dimly lit house and night scented garden in the small hours, what he means. I jerk back to the grim present. There is no garden here. No night lights. No comfortable white bathroom with knobby brass taps and long rails of fluffy multicoloured towels.

'Well,' Jonah continues, 'this tiny scruffy cat was in the kitchen when I came down, oh, a couple of nights ago it was. It must have come in through the cat flap. It was absolutely terrified of me, so I just put some milk down for it and left it and went back to bed. Then in the morning there was no sign of it and I thought maybe I had just dreamt it.'

'And the milk?'

'Well if it wasn't a dream, I suppose Mum must have cleared the milk away. She didn't say anything though.'

'Mm.'

Jonah starts to try and find his place in the encyclopaedia again and I sit and wonder what I can do about the cat. Nothing, probably. I have neither the cat itself nor the weird boy's real address. I am about to tell Jonah about the address the boy gave me when Mum comes breezing in through the door.

'Hi children! Hi! How was your day?'

'Fine thanks. There's tea in the pot,' mutters Jonah automatically, making no effort to hide the cigarette he has just lit from the stub of the previous one or to raise his eyes from his book.

Mum has tried everything to stop Jonah smoking, from lecturing him, to calmly explaining the health hazards, to buying him a pamphlet with pictures of

—— 24 ——

horribly blackened pickled lungs in it. Nothing has helped so far, even the time when she seized his pack of cigarettes and stamped on it. She never gives up though, and I have the feeling that he's due for another onslaught soon.

I start to search for the right words to explain just why Miss Patel will be calling round later this evening.

Dinner is hell. Mum is trying to understand but she keeps going back to the subject of why I took the day off school. She just can't seem to leave it alone.

'I know it hasn't been easy for you lately, Emily,' she says as she offers me more mince. I shake my head. I think I might become a vegetarian. 'What can we do to make you feel better?' She looks a bit desperate. She also looks very tired and disheartened.

I know she hates her job at Le Plastique, but she has to do it to pay the mortgage. She has taken defiantly to wearing lots of her beautiful antique jewellery to work, as a sort of gesture of scorn against what she has to sell. Today she is wearing her long, carved, politically incorrect ivory earrings. Once long ago, in happier days, Samantha looked silently aghast at the wearing of ivory and Mum said, 'If I don't wear them, then this elephant will have died in vain.'

Jonah started trying to explain that this was hardly logical, since wearing them might make everyone else want a pair too and then the hunters would go out and shoot lots more elephants, but Mum just said sharply, her voice rising, 'I like them. I just like them. Surely I can have *some* things that I like in this world! The rest of you do!'

I do have moments of sympathy for Mum. I have one now, as her spoonful of garlic and onion-scented mince hovers over my baked potato, a symbol of the real comfort she wishes she were able to give.

'I'll tell you what I thought,' she says, putting false brightness into her voice. 'I know we all miss Andromeda dreadfully. I thought we could get a pet. We *could* get another cat, but being so near the main road could be dangerous for it, so it might be better to get a dog, then we could take it for walks on a lead and let it go for runs in the park . . .'

'No!' Jonah shouts it, then looks very surprised at himself. 'No, let's get a cat. Two cats?' His voice trails off. He looks a bit sheepish and clasps his hands on the table and grins.

'Why?' Mum looks puzzled. 'I thought you particularly would like a dog, Jonah. You always used to say . . .'

At that moment Miss Patel arrives, tapping on the front door and calling out. Mum goes to let her in and I look at Jonah. It's true. He was always nagging about getting a dog at one time. He is looking rather flushed and confused.

'Don't ask,' he says. 'I don't know. I would much rather have a dog. I didn't mean to say that. I didn't know I was going to. I suppose it's with talking about that little black cat earlier. It was rather sweet . . .'

'Emily, Jonah, hello. I'm sorry to interrupt your meal,' says Miss Patel. Mum reassures her that we had just finished and we all go and sit at the other end of the room round the fireplace. Mum puts a match to the logs and coal in the grate and a wisp of smoke curls up.

Miss Patel talks about general things, the traumas of moving house, her holiday in India.

'How is your mother, Miss Patel?' asks Mum. 'I was so sorry when Emily told me she was seriously ill.'

'She has plague.' Miss Patel's voice is utterly bleak. 'It

is a big problem in India at the moment.' I sit up straight in shock. Miss Patel continues. 'She is very ill, but she will survive. We have every hope for that now. She has responded very well to the antibiotics. For a while, it was not so certain. A lot of the doctors had fled.'

She sighs, and the wind funnels down the chimney, a great hollow mockery of this thin woman's despair. The smoke eddies and swirls in the fireplace and the echo of the wind in the chimney billows across the flagstone floor to the stairwell. I feel unreal, and the room with its familiar furniture and people seems very far off. I lean back in my armchair and half close my eyes.

Miss Patel says a lot of comforting things about bad exam results. She tells us a funny story about when she did badly in her exams and her parents threatened her with an immediate arranged marriage and no consultation if she didn't improve. I have a strong feeling that it was nowhere near as funny at the time. She talks some more about her visit to India.

'My friend Alice Smith who runs the Hound Hill Museum came with me,' she says, turning to me. 'You should visit the museum, Emily. Have you been?' She has seen my sudden interest. 'No? You must. Maybe I'll take the whole class there one day soon.'

I have just remembered about the stone in the park, and I ask her about it. Miss Patel tilts her head. 'You mean the small memorial stone by the west wall? The one with a little fence round it which the museum maintains?'

For a moment I remember very vividly the stone, the great tree, the bare earth, the flurry of the frightened wren. 'Yes.'

Miss Patel nods. 'How strange you should have found that stone today, just when we are also talking about plague. It is a plague pit. That end of the park, near the church, the big wooded triangle, is the site of an old plague pit from the time of the Great Plague of London in 1665. Could you make out the inscription?'

'No.' I shake my head, listening intently, feeling strange.

'No, well it is not surprising. The only reason we do know exactly what it says is from records in the museum which date from the last century. Since then pollution has eroded the lettering so that it is really not legible any more. Let me think . . . it gives the date, 1665, then it says "To the sweet memory of six thousand and twenty souls".' She sighs again, and shakes her head. 'So many. One can scarcely contemplate it. So much sorrow. And of course it was only one of many such pits. Here, I shall write the inscription down for you so that you have the correct seventeenth-century spelling.' She whips out a notebook from her handbag and scribbles rapidly, then tears out the page and hands it to me.

1665
To the swete memorye of 6020 soules

'So many.' I repeat her words in a whisper. I think of the tree trunk vanishing into the earth where these people lie, linking the visible and invisible worlds.

'You should talk to Alice,' says Miss Patel. 'I can see that you are interested. She hasn't been feeling too well since we came back from India, but in a few days maybe. She and I were at college together. You'll like her.'

I nod, and manage a smile.

The wind is rising. I go to bed early, drained by the events of the day. I hear the shifting air in the chimney next to my wardrobe alcove. Mum has suggested a house-warming party. I feel guilty that she is going to such lengths to cheer me up. I don't want a party. I don't know anyone round here well enough to invite them. It will be embarrassing. Mum has already invited Miss Patel. No doubt Roger will be coming too.

I shuffle my quilt into a nest around me, listening to the sounds outside. I can hear the rattle of a train in the distance as the wind drops, and the rattle of the cat flap closer by as it rises again.

I think of the brown-eyed boy and his lost cat. I feel sorry for him, despite his strangeness. It is sad to lose an animal you love. I feel my mind slipping towards sleep. I briefly jump back into wakefulness and panic at the thought of Jonah in his room, innocent and unprotected from the things of the night. The growing gale whines and mews along the alleys and courtyards. Tiredness overtakes me and I sleep.

Six

I WAKE WITH A TERRIBLE START, AND THE DREAM still vivid in my head. The woman had been screaming, 'No, no, don't shut us in . . .' I can still hear her voice. Its echo is in the house. Not here, but outside my room, in the stairwell and in the chimney.

I hardly dare move. My face is turned to the wall. My room is in darkness, except for the faint light from the old-fashioned street lamp in the courtyard below.

I swivel my eyes and look over my shoulder. The dark shape of my dressing gown hangs on the door. The wardrobe looms in the alcove. The low beams jut across the ceiling, all barely visible in the darkness. The wind is still blowing outside, gusting and screaming like human voices, wild and unpredictable. I hear something metal go clanging down the street. No wonder I have been having nightmares.

That woman — I can still see her so clearly — she was in her thirties maybe, and dressed in clothes from long ago. I realise, as I think of her clothes, just what has conjured up this dream. It must be all the talk of plague and plague pits. I turn over and try to go back to sleep.

'Sarah . . .'

The voice is like a sigh. Like the wind itself. I sit up in shock. No! What is this? Then I realise that I must have drifted straight back to sleep and started dreaming again.

I stare across the room at the door. My dressing gown

looks like a person standing there. I jerk round as there seems to be a movement and a glimmer on the opposite side of the room now, near my dressing table, as if something crossed in front of the long mirror.

I try to think sensibly. Leaves and debris must be flying past the window, across the light from the courtyard lamp. I struggle for calmness. The nightmare feeling is still with me. I shall have to get up to make it go away.

Where we lived before, if I woke in the night, I knew that a stroll round the house and a mug of hot chocolate would send me off to sleep again. I feel wide awake now, but perhaps it will still work. I stretch out my hand — it feels utterly vulnerable in the blackness — and switch on my bedside lamp.

It is an immense relief to have the light on. I get out of bed and switch the main lights on and my dressing table lamp too. I turn my clock radio on — it is playing something by The Levellers — and swig down the remains of an old, cold cup of tea. This all feels much better. I put my slippers and dressing gown on and go downstairs, wondering when we will be able to afford an electrician to install a light on the landing.

The stairs creak — I feel it beneath my feet — but the wind is drowning out all sound. I am several steps into the dark living room, reaching for the light switch, before I realise that I am not alone. I suppress a gasp. Someone is there, over on the far side of the room, moving about in the gloom. I feel myself go rigid. The roots of my hair prickle and the skin of my scalp seems to creep on my skull. I cannot move.

I try to think. It cannot be Mum or Jonah, because they would have switched the lights on. Can those sounds and shadowy movements be a trick of the wind? No, there is an animal purposefulness about them.

Might it be the little cat come back to escape the wild weather? No, this is something larger. It can only be a burglar, over there by the television set, video player and music centre, the things he would be likely to steal.

I look over towards the pale shape of the telephone on the small table by the door. Can I reach it to dial 999 before the intruder sees me? No, he would hear the clicks and beeps as I lifted the receiver and dialled, and anyway it is too dark to see what I am doing. He would just rush straight across the room at me. For all I know he might be armed.

I am trembling with tension and I have a stomach ache. Maybe I should go upstairs and get Mum or Jonah, but then there isn't a telephone up there, and it might endanger them too. Perhaps I should just let him steal the stuff rather than risking any of us being attacked.

There is a bump and a dragging sound. I have to take action of some sort. I switch the lights on.

The figure whips round.

'Ah!' he croaks, ducking his head away from the light, dazzled. It is the young man from the alley. My first feeling is one of intense disappointment. So he's just a thief. He was checking out the place, yesterday. He has the video recorder in his arms.

'Put that down!' I astonish myself by the ferocity in my voice. My breath is fluttering in my throat like a little bird, but the feeling of loss I experience at the knowledge that he is no more than a shameful burglar gives me strength. He is staring at me.

'I have drunk too much,' he whispers, looking me up and down. This infuriates me. So he's going to blame his dishonesty on drink. How pathetic. I point at the video recorder he is holding. He looks at it as if puzzled as to how it got there.

'This is a great mystery,' he says.

Maybe he really is drunk. If so I must be extra careful. He could be even more dangerous than if he were sober.

'Put it down,' I repeat. He obeys me, putting the machine on the sofa.

'Who are you?' he asks. I feel as if this should be my line. I start edging my way round the room to get at one of the pokers in the kitchen range, in case I might need to defend myself.

'Mind your own business. I think you'd better get out of here before I call the police.'

'What do you mean? You know we can no longer go out . . .' His accent is as strange as ever but I am used to it now. It is almost as if it were a way of speaking that I once knew and now have forgotten. I must keep him talking and calm until I can persuade him out of the house. I wonder how he got in. I must not let it occur to him to attack me. I want to scream 'Help! Help! Burglar!' but that might provoke him to shut me up by violent means.

Suddenly he comes towards me fast. I recoil.

'I cannot understand these things . . . perhaps I am dreaming. I seek my cat and I find you, and these . . .' He gestures behind him to the television, video and music centre. 'Perhaps this is the madness that comes with the sickness. Perhaps I too am now doomed, despite all my care.' He shakes his head. 'It is what I deserve . . .' He is standing right in front of me now. He smells musty, of hedgerows and the farm. It occurs to me that he may be completely mad and that I might be in far greater danger than I had ever imagined. I cannot understand how he can be so different from the smiling boy of yesterday. He seems a different person now, unstable and confused. What does all this mean?

'Look, I'm sure you don't deserve to be doomed. You just deserve to be in prison.'

'I am imprisoned. Yes, I am imprisoned.' He rubs his hands over his face. There is a frightening, desperate look in his eyes, and none of the humour of yesterday. 'Yet imprisonment is nothing beside that worse punishment which is in my mind, the knowledge of what I did. I shall never recover from that.' He stops, then adds after a moment, 'Never. Have you been sent to haunt me? Is it you who haunts my sleep and gives me these dreams?' I stare at him. I really don't understand what is happening. Could he be a sleepwalker? The thought suddenly occurs to me. I have sleepwalked myself in the past and it is very disorientating.

I take a step nearer to the kitchen and he steps with me, closer still. I have no idea how I should reply to him. Perhaps I should just keep him talking.

'My brother saw your cat. It came into our kitchen a few nights ago.'

The transformation in him is shocking. His eyes widen and his mouth opens in a silent 'Oh'.

'He saw him? He saw Pardoner, my cat?' The young man grabs me by the arms and I give a tiny shriek and flinch away. He lets go of me and says, 'Forgive me, lady. Is it really true then, that he is not dead? Pardoner is not dead? Your brother has truly seen him? You are not the instrument of God's design to punish me, by giving me false hope?'

'Well, my brother saw a cat that sounds like yours. That's all I can tell you really. He gave it some milk but it was gone by morning.'

The intruder looks over towards the front door and his lips tremble. 'Where can he be? He could be anywhere out there, lost. He will be hungry. He will not be able to understand. He will never come back to me now.' He sinks his head into his hands. I feel pity for him, and a great desire to comfort him, insane as he clearly is. His

— 34 —

next words strip away all my sympathy.

'They said it was necessary, to kill. Whichever choice I made was wrong . . . there was no right way. Now I know I shall never recover from it, not for all eternity. We have been enclosed here so long, ever since the baker's wife fell ill. The watchmen guard us front and back and we are all so tired . . . so tired . . . When the madness comes it will be welcome. I shall greet it as a friend, for I cannot go on.'

The shock takes a moment to hit me. Kill. Did he say kill? I find that I am shaking quite violently. I step to the side, over the threshold of the kitchen now. He looks back across the room towards the video recorder on the sofa, and at last I can reach the poker, the long iron poker with the goat's head handle. Next to me the wind bellows into the fireplace of the range and lifts the ash.

'I'm so tired,' the boy repeats, and I can hardly hear him. He closes his eyes for a second, and I quietly take hold of the poker and raise it high, but I cannot hit him, and when he opens his eyes and sees what I am doing his expression changes and he grabs my arm and twists it down so that the poker clangs from my grasp on to the tiles of the hearth.

Now I scream. I fill my lungs and fight him and fill the kitchen with screaming. In the moment that I tear myself from his grip and stagger so that my head smashes against the corner of the mantelpiece, I hear Jonah's voice on the staircase calling, 'Emily? Emily, is that you? Ae you all right?'

Then the kitchen whirls up in front of me and goes black.

Seven

I AM AWARE OF BEING CARRIED TO THE LIVING room, of Mum and Jonah propping me against the cushions of the sofa.

'. . . sleepwalking again . . .' I hear Mum say.

'It's ages since she did that, isn't it, Mum?'

'Mm.' Mum sounds distracted. 'It's probably all the upsets, you know, the move and everything.'

My head hurts. I open my eyes then close them again, dazzled, as the boy was earlier. Mum peers into my face.

'I'm going to ring for an ambulance, Em. How do you feel? You've given your head a nasty bump.'

'Mum . . .' My voice will only come out faintly, and the effort of speaking makes my head knock. 'Mum . . . the burglar . . . Has he escaped? Did he get away?' I try to look round but I am unable to move my head.

'What?' Mum looks horrified and stands up to stare all round the room. Jonah rushes into the kitchen and I can hear him searching, opening the larder and pulling the curtains back to check the windows.

I hear them talking.

'. . . no, nobody . . . couldn't have got past me to go upstairs . . .'

'. . . maybe a dream while she was sleepwalking . . .'

'The video *was* on the sofa, Mum. Remember? I had to move it so we could put Emily there.'

'Oh, I put it there earlier, Jonah, when I was trying to set the timer and I wanted to see properly.' She looks at me anxiously. 'Emily, you can tell us more about the burglar in a minute. It must have been a dream, darling. I'm just going to ring for an ambulance now. We need to get your head seen to.'

These words are to come back to me often over the next few hours, days and weeks.

I have mild concussion but not, as Mum feared, a cracked skull.

When we reach the hospital I am rushed past a lot of people who look as if they have been waiting for ages. My head wound is examined and x-rayed. The doctors and nurses are kind, and careful with my increasingly painful bump. My vision and reflexes are tested, my blood pressure and pulse taken. A bandage is wound round my head. I look like Tutankhamun on a bad day.

When we arrive back home the first light of dawn is fading the sky to patchy blue, like stonewashed jeans. Chimneys stand out against it all the way up the hill. They look like prison bars, or rotten teeth, or organ pipes. No, they look like the pipes of some other, unknown instrument.

Mum and I find that Jonah has searched the house from top to bottom. Nothing is missing. Nothing is out of place. There are no signs of forced entry. I receive pitying stares and understanding hugs from both Mum and Jonah. Ignoring their efforts to get me to bed I go and stand first in the living room, where earlier I faced the young man, then in the kitchen by the big black range, where I seized the poker.

I can imagine him. I can hear his voice echoing in my mind. I can remember his crazed misery. He used language in ways which I would not have invented, even in a dream. We all know what dreams are like, don't we, even waking dreams, even sleepwalking dreams. We also know what a solid, slightly smelly human being standing in our own kitchen is like. They are not the same.

Mum bustles round and makes cups of tea. Jonah checks the locks again. He comes to stand in front of me as I sink on to the living room sofa. The wind is dropping now but a leftover gust roars unexpectedly down the chimney. Briefly a burnt-out chunk of Coalite glows pink again, before fading instantly back into bone-coloured dust. Jonah looks into my eyes rather as the casualty doctor did, suspicious, anticipating the worst.

'He was here,' I say. 'It was that boy who was looking for his cat.'

'You saw him clearly?' Jonah is speaking quietly. He doesn't want Mum to hear. I can hear cups clattering in the kitchen.

'Yes. I talked to him.'

'Did he hit you?'

We have already been through this at the hospital, whether or not someone hit me. I repeat what I said then, because I cannot be certain that I wasn't sleepwalking. I cannot be certain that I wouldn't have fallen anyway, whether or not the boy had grabbed me. There is one other inescapable fact too. I was the first one to threaten violence. It was my fault. I cannot get away from that.

'No.'

Jonah frowns. 'Do you know where we haven't checked? We haven't checked the chimney yet.'

My heart gives a thump. The chimney, the place of sounds and whispering, is a yawning gap behind Jonah's back. Both this fireplace and the kitchen range have chimneys leading into the same large outer chimney, shared with next door. This hearth is huge, disproportionate to the room. The estate agent said parts of it were Elizabethan, when she showed us round. She said small sections were parts of the original walls of a much older building incorporated into a new cottage for factory workers with the coming of the industrial revolution.

The boy could probably have climbed up this chimney. The hearth in the kitchen, blocked by its later Victorian range, would have been more difficult.

Awkwardly Jonah stoops and peers up the sooty tunnel. He emerges with black smudges on his cheeks, shaking his head. 'Impossible, unless he was a child or a dwarf. It gets narrow very quickly. So he certainly couldn't have gone up the kitchen one.' He glances round the living room once more. 'You say he was stealing the video? Maybe we should check in case he's damaged it.'

I am grateful to Jonah for humouring me, even if he is unable actually to believe me. He switches the television and video recorder on, pressing 'Rewind' then 'Play' without checking whatever it was that Mum recorded earlier. The screen fizzes white then crackles before clearing to show a woman in a long dress. She is sitting on a beautifully carved chair, her face bent down and away from the camera, playing some sort of round-backed stringed instrument.

The notes sob on the air, almost speaking the words before the camera pans back to reveal the profile of a man who begins singing. He has a pure, high voice.

> *'Alas my love*
> *You do me wrong*
> *To cast me off*
> *Discourteously . . .'*

Mum comes in with a loaded tray. 'I thought we might like some chocolate cake too ... Oh, how lovely, "Greensleeves". Is this on now? It seems a strange thing to have on at five o'clock in the morning.'

'It's what you recorded earlier, Mum,' says Jonah, taking the tray from her. Mum shakes her head as she clears a space on the coffee table.

'No, I recorded the film on Channel Four. There was nothing like this on.'

'Rewind it.' They both stare at me and I realise how overemphatic I must have sounded. 'Please. Please just play it again.'

Without argument Jonah presses 'Rewind'. The tape clicks off immediately. He tries again. The same thing happens. The tape will not rewind. With a sigh of irritation Jonah ejects the tape and looks at it. He frowns, puzzled, then holds the cassette out to me, tilting it so that I can see. I have started to feel very cold even before I understand what he is showing me. The tape will not rewind because it is already at the very beginning. It has not played.

'Play it,' I whisper. Jonah reinserts the cassette and presses 'Play'. The music for the film starts at once. The titles are just rolling up. I sit up and grab the remote control and flick round the television stations one after the other. There is no music of any sort.

'You saw it, didn't you?' I look back and forth between Jonah and Mum. My voice sounds hoarse and unnatural, but I can't help that. 'You saw it and heard it, didn't you? "Greensleeves"?'

They both nod. I subside against the cushions.

'Why?' whispers Jonah. 'Why does it matter? It's just a fault of some sort. Probably something to do with the timer.'

Mum smiles in bewilderment at the state I am

obviously in. 'It was just an advert, or a trailer for something, Em. It wasn't something on the tape. Why is it upsetting you? Anyway, it's gone now . . .'

That is when we hear the cat flap click.

Eight

*T*HE SMALL BLACK CAT WALKS SLOWLY INTO THE room. We are all frozen into the positions we were in when the cat flap clicked. My shocked stillness seems to have immobilised everyone. I watch the tiny furry creature cross the floor, and the oddness is that it *is* furry, solid and real, because in the last few moments I have finally allowed into my brain the word that could not be said before. The word ghost.

'Oh!' says Mum. Her tone is very tender. She bends and holds out her hand. The cat starts to rush up to her, then stops and cowers, as if struck by sudden fear. It is scarcely more than a kitten. Mum kneels down where she is and says, 'It's all right. It's all right, cat. We won't hurt you.' She is talking in a quiet voice and smiling.

For a strange moment I feel as if I can remember being a baby. I feel as if she is talking to me and that I am tiny and helpless. I am struck by a terrible wave of longing. It is like slipping back in time, it is so real.

When I recover I see that the kitten has crept forward and has started rubbing its tiny triangular face against Mum's fingers. It is completely black and I see now that it is shockingly thin. Its fur is patchy, rough and worn away on one shoulder. There is the scar of an old injury on its head. It has started purring loudly. Mum gathers it up in her arms and kisses its head and whispers, 'Poor thing. Look how thin it is. It's starving. I must get it some food.'

Because she obviously doesn't want to put it down, Jonah smiles and goes into the kitchen. I can hear him clanking around with dishes and milk bottles.

'Let me see it, Mum,' I say. She brings it over to me. I move up so that she can sit on the edge of the sofa. As she sits down the cat burrows into the folds of her cardigan and its eyelids begin to droop. I stretch out my hand and touch it. It is warm, shaggily rough, vibrating with the violence of its purring. For the first time since I hit my head, in fact only for the second time since we moved here, I find that I am crying.

Jonah comes in with a saucer of milk and a dish of chopped up chicken leftovers. He is not usually so domestic. He tilts his head and gives a supportive grimace when he sees that I am crying. I realise abruptly that one day soon Jonah is going to be quite grown up, someone who can possibly make life feel better, at times when such a person is needed.

Mum strokes the black kitten's bald, scarred head and puts the tiny creature down in front of the food. It wobbles and just stares at the two dishes for a moment, then it launches itself at the milk. There are slurpy lapping sounds. White droplets fly all over the carpet. The milk is gone. The cat's face is dripping. Then it falls over. Its little legs just give way.

Mum jumps up in concern, but it is struggling to its feet again, heading for the chicken now. The chicken is too much for it, though. It pushes its face in amongst the pieces and licks at the jelly, but it does not attempt to eat the meat.

Mum kneels down again and peers closely at it. 'We'll just have to keep it on liquids to start off with,' she says after a moment. 'The poor thing is severely malnourished. It's like when people are starving, you know. They can only have drinks for a while until their bodies are able to cope again.' She turns to look at Jonah and me. 'I'm going to make this cat better, children. I think we've found our pet.'

'But . . .' Jonah sits on the arm of the sofa, looking concerned. 'Emily said it belonged to that boy, the one who came to the door.'

Mum gives him an incredulous look. '*Anyone* who lets an animal get into this sort of state isn't fit to own one.'

'But Mum,' I put in weakly. 'It had run away. He had lost it. He was dreadfully concerned and he was searching for it. Even if it was only a dream that I saw him in the house tonight, he really was at the back door the other day. We ought to tell the police and the RSPCA that we've found his cat, in case he has reported it missing.'

Mum compresses her lips. 'No. Absolutely not. I don't like the sound of that young man at all. There must have been something unsavoury about him to make you dream he was a burglar, Emily. Anyway, this cat has old scars.' She picks it up again and settles into an armchair with it on her lap. 'Look at its head. These marks are probably a result of long term ill-treatment. If that lad comes back I'll see what he's like and maybe I'll talk to him about it, but for now the cat stays here.'

I know that tone of voice. It's the one that said no John, there's no point in keeping on trying to mend our marriage. None at all. Absolutely not.

So we don't argue with her any further, and secretly I am glad.

It is a bright morning with sunlight pouring in through the windows when I finally go back to bed. A blackbird is singing wildly in the courtyard. I sink down under the quilt. My head throbs gently on the pillow as I close my eyes and try to sleep. Something touches my cheek. It is like a breath, but I realise that the window is open and that the breeze must have reached me.

It takes me a long time to go to sleep. I hear Jonah go to school, then Mum go out, and ten minutes later come back in again. I hear Roger next door whistling on his doorstep. He whistles pop songs but he always gets them slightly wrong, which is very annoying. I hear Mrs Bagling the other side talking to the milkman, arguing about her bill. I drift into sleep, wake, then drift again.

I dream about the boy, but it is just an ordinary dream, a remembering dream, not vivid and real like last night's dream about the woman. His sadness is gentler than last night, more like it was earlier, in the alley. It is a slow, deep-running melancholy, far below the surface. I wake briefly again, then go back to sleep.

The shock makes me cry out loud. I am in Jonah's room, and the boy is in the corner. It is night. A candle burns under the window. I must have slept a long time.

He is sitting on a low stool and in his hands is a large slab of granite. It is dripping with blood. It is the stone which stands outside our back door, the roughly conical chunk of Lakeland green granite that was already there when we arrived at this house. Mum uses it as a doorstop when she wants to prop the back door open and let the steam out of the kitchen.

The young man does not speak. Although I am so close to him he does not take any notice of me. A drop of blood from the stone falls on to one of his boots. He turns his head and stares away out of the window. The window is different from normal, smaller, with thick, rounded, greenish glass that gives off faint rainbow hues in the candlelight. There is none of Jonah's furniture here, just the low stool on which the boy is sitting, a cupboard, a

—— 45 ——

high-backed carved chair and a wooden bed piled with soft-looking cream woollen blankets.

A tear wells out of the inner corner of the boy's left eye and runs down beside his nose. I am swamped with pity. I have to speak to him, though it feels as if there is a barrier stopping me, a barrier of something like fog, or the blurring that occurs with great distance. I doubt the ability of my voice to make enough sound, and of his ears to hear it.

'We have found your cat.' I force the words out.

He looks in my direction, narrowing his eyes and peering. At last he shakes his head and shrugs.

'If there is someone there, you should go,' he rasps in a voice that has recently been crying. 'For if you do not, then you might be the next one to be killed. What is one more, after all? What is one more this day, after so many?'

As he speaks, I see the blood on the wall beside him, a splattered stain, running bright red still, where Jonah's chest of drawers had stood.

'Emily!' Someone is shaking me. 'Emily! Wake up! Oh Roger, help me. I know you're not supposed to wake sleepwalkers but we can't just let her stand here screaming.'

A great jolt shakes me, like an electric shock. I actually see the room and the boy recede, hurtling into the distance as if down a tunnel, and I am in Jonah's room with my own screams still echoing in my ears.

Mum and Roger each have an arm round me and are helping me along like an invalid, past Jonah's wardrobe and desk and heaps of discarded clothing.

'Poor Emily. Come along now. Let's get you back to bed,' says Roger jauntily.

I have no warning of what I am going to do. It is not a conscious decision. It just happens. I swear at him. In words of rage and brevity I recommend that he should depart. He lets go of me as if I had suddenly become radioactive, and even Mum briefly loosens her grip.

'Emily!' she gasps, then she groans and hugs me. 'Oh dear, it's all right. You can't help it. It's the shock. I shouldn't have woken you . . .'

'Well!' says Roger. 'Well!' and he stamps off down the stairs.

'Oh Roger, please, I'm sorry. Emily didn't mean it. Don't go . . .'

I am awake now. 'Sorry, Mum. I did mean it, but sorry.'

'Oh Em . . .' She hugs me again. 'It will get better. I promise. I *know* you're having a terrible time just now, but once we've settled in here, once you get used to the new school and you get to know lots of people round here, you really will feel better. And now we've got Timmy . . .'

I stop abruptly on the threshold of my room. 'Timmy?'

'Yes, our little cat. I thought we could call him Timmy.' Mum smiles a smile of combined hope and uncertainty. I feel for her a trace of the pity I felt for the young man. I glance behind me towards Jonah's room, then I look back at Mum.

'The cat's name is Pardoner,' I say gently. 'Pardoner, that is what it is called. Try it. I think you'll find it will answer to that.'

'Pardoner?' Mum looks puzzled. 'That's a peculiar name for a cat. You mean, like "The Pardoner's Tale" from Chaucer's *Canterbury Tales*? Like the pardoners in the Middle Ages who sold people pardons for their sins?'

'Well, I suppose so.'

'Did that young man tell you this when he came to the back door yesterday?'

I nod and am about to say yes, when I realise that it was not then. It was not then at all. It was last night.

I reach my dressing gown down from my bedroom door and put it on because now I am shivering and my arms and legs feel full of icicles. If the cat knows its name, it means one thing. Last night was real.

Nine

'I THINK WE HAD BETTER INVITE ALL THE neighbours,' says Mum later as we sit at the kitchen table drinking coffee. It is her day off work and she seems to be in a good mood. 'They made us so welcome when we moved here. It would be a little thank you. I don't think I've ever known such a friendly neighbourhood. Even though the people are all so different it's as if they had something in common.'

I sigh, thinking of our neighbours.

'I invited Roger earlier, and Miss Patel is coming.' Mum ticks two names on the list in front of her. 'If you feel up to it we'll go and see Mrs Bagling in a minute. You can start thinking which school friends you would like to invite.'

I look through the kitchen doorway into the living room where the cat is sleeping next to the hearth. The fire is not lit, but a patch of sunlight from the tall front window which looks out on to the street is shining on the faded tan and rose coloured hearth rug.

I have not tried out the name Pardoner on it yet. I try to tell myself that it is because the poor bedraggled thing is sleeping, but really I do not have the courage.

If the cat knows its name, and if last night was real, we have either had a burglar in the house, or a ghost. I do not want either to be the case.

Mum sees where I am looking.

'You know, you might have misheard that boy, Emily, when he told you the cat's name. Anyway, cats often don't answer to their names. We could call it anything and it would soon get used to it. It's very young. I don't mind if you *want* to call it Pardoner, but I don't think it's going to have a nervous breakdown if we call it something else. Anyway, try it out. Go on. Let's see if it responds. I'll tell you what, let's try a different name first as a sort of control test. Sometimes they'll react to anything you say in a certain tone of voice, particularly if they think it means food.'

She goes into the living room and sits on the arm of the sofa. It used to be a crime-of-crimes to sit on the arms of the furniture when we lived at our old house. It suddenly strikes me that a lot of the rules have been relaxed since we moved.

I watch them through the doorway.

'Attila, oh Attila?' calls Mum with a grin. The cat continues sleeping. She softens her voice into a cooing, honeyed tone. 'Genghis darling. Genghis Khan, wake up.' Still the cat does not stir.

I am having to laugh despite myself, even though laughter hurts my head. In the same voice Mum calls, 'Pardoner, oh Pardoner, little kitten, wake up now . . .'

Nothing happens. The cat continues sleeping. Outside, the rag-and-bone man goes by once more with his unrhythmic bell ringing. He is shouting something as well this time, but I cannot tell what, something like 'Bring out old beds'. At the same time there is a sound in the kitchen, close to where I sit with my back to the kitchen range. I recognise it at once. It is the scuttering noise I heard yesterday when I switched on the television set. I spin round in my chair. Nothing. The grate is empty except for old cinders. The sound comes again.

'Mum . . .' I whisper it. 'Mum, theres's something in the chimney . . .'

She turns her attention away from the cat and comes back into the kitchen.

'What?'

Then it appears. First we see nose and whiskers. They are twitching at the far corner of the fireplace opening. Both Mum and I remain absolutely still. A face emerges, long pointed nose, pink and cleft at the tip, satellite dish ears, eyes like raisins. It edges out, looking round. I had not known I could be so still. It is big, as big as the kitten, but this is no kitten. At last it stands in the middle of the hearth, scythe-backed, with sleek grey and black mottled fur and tiny pink feet. A flat, sour smell fills the kitchen and seems to lie on my tongue like the taste of overripe cheese.

Mum is the first to utter a sound. She does not scream; it is more of a strangled gurgle.

'Dear Lord, a rat . . .'

With truly amazing reflexes she grabs the goat's head poker and lashes out at it. Amid a rattle of falling soot the creature is gone, back up the chimney, its extraordinarily long tail whipping after it, and Mum and I are left standing by the hearth, shaking.

'Oh . . . oh . . .' Mum is visibly shocked. I do not have time to be though, because now there is another sound. It is coming from the living room. It is high-pitched, ghastly, unidentifiable. I tiptoe through the open doorway in horrified anticipation, looking from left to right. The sound quietens until it suddenly becomes recognisable, a thin mewing, insubstantial as the wind in the alleys, coming from the patch of sunshine on the rug.

The cat is dreaming. Its paws are twitching and the shrill, hungry sound is coming from its open mouth. I move closer. Its eyes are turned up, revealing moon crescents of white, flickering and crazy.

I watch it and I wonder, what has this cat seen? What has it been through? What is it seeing now?

I kneel down and stroke it.

'It's all right,' I whisper. 'Shh. Poor cat. Poor thing.' It is warm. Its fur has soaked up the sun. This is no ghost cat so it cannot have a ghost master. I run my thumb over its ridged head, between its ears. 'Pardoner? Is that your name? Poor old Pardoner, you're in a worse state than I am.'

Mum appears by my side with a new saucer of milk. The cat opens its eyes and struggles to its feet, and whether it gets up for its name or for the milk, it is impossible to tell.

Before we go out to see the neighbours Mum telephones the pest control people and arranges for them to come round tomorrow.

'Rats! Ugh!' she mutters as she hangs up the receiver. 'Roger's mice are bad enough, but rats!'

As we set off to issue our invitations, I decide that if I see the strange boy again, I might even invite *him* to our party. If he is a burglar, maybe he can be reformed. I cannot get his misery out of my mind; it so much chimed with my own. I feel I can understand someone being driven to crime by sheer unhappiness or loss.

I feel guilty that we have his cat. He wanted so desperately to find it. As we knock at the door of our neighbour on the opposite side of us from Roger, the feeling grows in me that whatever it takes, I must find the boy. I realise that I don't even know his name, but judging by the odd address he gave, it seems possible that he might live somewhere round here. I decide to ask Mrs Bagling.

At first glance Mrs Bagling doesn't look like a party-going person. She calls out to us to come in, and we find her sitting in a pink velvet chair by a large, smoking fire. She is wearing heavy make-up and a frilly pink dress and is rocking to and fro silently in her chair.

'My dears!' She extends a hand flaming with jewels. 'How delightful. Would you care for a glass of sherry?'

Mum accepts with a pleased smile and sits down in one of several more pink velvet chairs. Mrs Bagling has long grey hair down to her shoulders, but now she winds it up into a large bun and spears it into place with two glittering hairpins. She totters to her feet and pours sticky brown sherry for all three of us, before I can protest.

She and Mum chat for a while and she accepts our party invitation with obvious delight.

'Oh, what fun. It's ages since we've had a party on Hound Hill. Everyone's so short of money these days, and what with . . .' She stops abruptly.

'What?' Mum prompts her, looking curious.

There is an awkward pause. Mrs Bagling shakes her head and looks uncomfortable. 'What with . . . what with such changeable weather . . .'

This is obviously not what she had been going to say, but we do not press her. I ask her about the boy in the coat and boots, though Mum looks as if she would prefer me not to. Mrs Bagling shakes her head.

'No dear, I can't say I know of anyone like that, and I do know most of the people round here. Like that poor Alice Smith up at the top of the hill. Did you hear about her? They came for her this morning.'

It takes me a moment to place the name, then I remember, Miss Patel's friend who runs the museum, the one who hasn't been too well since coming back from India.

'*Came* for her?' asks Mum, leaning forward in fascination.

Mrs Bagling lowers her voice and narrows her eyes. 'They say . . .' and here she glances over her shoulder and lays her hand on Mum's wrist. 'They say she picked up something nasty in India. They say that the men who came with the ambulance this morning were covered from head to foot in protective clothing, face masks, the lot. I heard from Mrs Rodriguez over the road that it was a special ambulance they took her away in too, all sealed up with double airlock doors.' She compresses her lips and nods. 'Rule Britannia, I say, and you can keep your nasty foreign diseases.'

After we leave Mrs Bagling we call on more neighbours on both sides of the road and invite them to our party, then we go home and I sleep through a dream-free afternoon.

Later I wake to the sound of the Evening Standard coming through the letter box. As I shamble downstairs looking for tea and biscuits, its headline faces me on the mat. 'PLAGUE HITS LONDON'.

Ten

THE RAT CATCHER ARRIVES EARLY THE NEXT morning. He is a big, red-faced man. He parks his fluorescent yellow van with 'Pest Destruction Guaranteed' emblazoned in black lettering, on the pavement outside our house. Perhaps he could be persuaded to deal with Roger next, I reflect nastily. He nods to Jonah who opens the door for him, and marches in carrying a box of poison, a small metal cage and a baseball bat.

'Sometimes we find the direct method's the best one,' he explains chillingly as he sees us staring at the bat. Jonah shudders and lights another cigarette, coughing wheezily and gasping for breath as he flaps his hand towards the kitchen to show the man where to go.

The rat catcher stares at him disapprovingly. 'That's not very healthy, you know, laddie. Your body should be a temple.' He hefts the baseball bat in both muscular hands and looks round suspiciously, as if expecting rats to be staring at him from every corner. Mum comes out of the kitchen in her dressing gown.

'Oh hello. Thank you so much for coming. I can't tell you how horrified we were to find we had a rat. This way.' She leads him into the kitchen. 'It was in the chimney. It was greyish-black, and *this* big.' She shows him with her hands. 'And that's not counting its tail which was about twice as long as the rest of it. Ugh.' She gives a grimace of distaste.

The man utters a patronising laugh and sits himself on the edge of the kitchen table next to the cornflakes. 'Three things, madam. It won't be *a* rat. It will be rats. They don't just come in ones, you know. Secondly, its tail certainly wouldn't have been longer than its body. You only get that with the black rat, and the black rat, Rattus Rattus to give it its technical name that we rodent control operatives use, has been virtually extinct in this country for many a long year. Dear me yes. Black rat, heh heh, now I've heard it all. It would be a *brown* rat, madam, Rattus Norvegicus. Its colour might have been greyish, but it would have been brownish-greyish. Even when the colour's similar you can tell because the brown rat has small flat ears and a tail shorter than its body . . .'

'It had great big ears and a tail longer than its body . . .' Mum interrupts, but the rat catcher isn't listening.

' . . . thirdly, it wouldn't be living in the *chimney* because brown rats can't climb. Now black rats, they could climb, by Jove they could climb, straight up a wall they'd go, but not yer brown rat, they're *ground* rats, and they're the ones that infest this area, so you see, stands to reason, it wouldn't be living in the chimney, would it madam? Probably hid in the hearth when you scared it.'

Mum's expression has cooled dramatically, but the rat catcher seems unaware of the danger he is in.

'Now madam,' he goes on, 'what we need to establish is where these *brown* rats are getting in. Where have you found traces of them, droppings and chewed wires and food interfered with, that sort of thing? Then we'll block up their way in and we'll poison the lot of them!' He gives a wild laugh and waves his baseball bat in the air. 'Unless I meet them face to face first! Heh heh.'

Mum is staring at him in silent incredulity. Suddenly

he leans forward and thrusts his face at her. 'You've got to be quick in this game, you know. Quick and fit. That lad of yours couldn't do it, coughing and spluttering like he is. Sounds as if *he's* been up the chimney. Heh heh.'

I am beginning to feel that the rat catcher is considerably more alarming than the rats. However now Mum has her hands on her hips and is standing very straight. I consider warning him, but instead Jonah and I exchange a glance, smile, and remain silent.

'Have you quite finished?' Mum enquires in a gentle voice, then continues without giving the rat catcher time to reply. 'Thank you so much for the lecture. Now please get off the kitchen table when I'm speaking to you, and put that bat down. Now let me see if I can put it simply. The rat was greyish-black, completely black in patches not brown or greyish-brown or brownish-grey or sky blue pink.'

She picks a piece of cold half-burnt coal out of the fireplace and places in in the rat catcher's hand, now divested of its bat. 'This colour. Got it? Its tail was about twice the length of its body and it had great big Mickey Mouse ears. This *black rat* came down the chimney and then it went back up again. If, as you say, black rats are climbers, then presumably that would be why it chose to climb. Now I'd like you to get rid of it for me, this black rat which my daughter and I saw and which came down the chimney and then climbed back up again.'

She smiles and pours herself a cup of tea. 'Do you think you can manage that? We haven't seen any droppings or traces, and we have only seen the one rat. As you may have heard, there is a case of plague in our street, which is naturally very worrying for everyone. You may know that in past centuries black rats spread plague right across Europe. They killed millions of people. That seems a very good reason for getting on with your job and getting rid of this one for us. Thank you so much.'

She turns to Jonah and me. 'Get ready for school, please. You're going to be late.'

As we cross the living room and head for the stairs I glance back to see the rat catcher rubbing his hands nervously down the sides of his trousers and looking rather shocked. I reflect that I haven't heard Mum on such form since her 'John, who precisely is this *Carmel*?' speech, after which she started crying rather a lot and stopped telling people off so stylishly. I feel a strange, comforting sense of normality returning as I climb the stairs, and I resist it, angry with myself and unwilling to believe that this place can contain anything of comfort or normality.

Five minutes later Mum comes upstairs carrying Pardoner under her arm. 'He'll have to stay up here all day, the rat catcher says, because of the poison in the kitchen. Shut him in when you leave, will you please?'

I take the kitten from her and give her a kiss on the cheek. She looks amazed and touched, and strokes my hair before going off to her own bedroom.

Pardoner has never been upstairs before. Now he explores my room with interest. I go downstairs and bring his food and drink dishes and litter tray up. Then I play with him for a while, aware that I ought to be getting ready. I trail a sock across the floor and he chases it and jumps on it from corners. He is still weak, and quite often staggers and falls over if he misjudges a manoeuvre, but he is behaving much more like a normal cat. Somehow this makes me feel that, unusually, this might turn out to be a good day, that it might even be that longed for thing, an ordinary day.

By the time we leave for school it is clear that this is not going to be an ordinary day at all. There are television vans in the street. Jonah and I watch the BBC vans move slowly up the hill towards Alice Smith's house and the Hound Hill Museum. I have still never been up that end of the hill myself.

Neighbours are coming out and standing on their doorsteps and exchanging expressions of astonishment. Roger comes out and speaks to Jonah but not to me. We go off to school amid a buzz of talk and supposition.

At lunchtime I go with two girls from my class to eat lunch in the park, and there we find a man with cameras slung all over him taking pictures of the area of the plague pit, at the direction of a woman who is jotting notes in a reporter's notebook.

By late afternoon, when Jonah and I arrive home, Mrs Bagling is in the living room with Mum. They are turning the television on and Mum says 'Shh!'

'A mediaeval disease is back in our midst . . .' begins the bespectacled science correspondent.

'Any dead rats yet?' enquires Jonah, looking towards the kitchen.

'Shh!' Mum repeats. 'The street's going to be on the telly. They interviewed Roger.'

I groan.

'Oh well, they would, wouldn't they,' mutters Jonah, settling down nevertheless to watch with interest.

It turns out that several other suspected plague cases, besides Alice, have been rushed to hospital on their arrival at Heathrow Airport from India. Alice's case, however, has been the only one where the sufferer has actually settled back at home and mixed with other people. All those with whom she has had contact are being screened. I wonder if this will include Miss Patel and whether it might mean no more sociology lessons for a while.

The presenter talks about the symptoms of plague,

how it starts with sickness and headache, then high fever accompanied by shivering and thirst, dark coloured marks with inflamed edges that appear on the skin, bleeding from the nose and mouth then agonising swellings in the armpits, neck and thighs, and the possibility of a wide range of other distressing symptoms. A historian from London University gives some historical background. Mum was right, in past times plague was carried by black rats coming off ships from other countries. The fleas on the rats sucked their infected blood then bit and infected other animals and human beings. I notice Mum give a great involuntary shiver as a picture of a black rat comes on the screen. It is exactly like the one we saw. So much for 'virtually extinct' — not on Hound Hill anyway.

The historian goes on to tell how during the Great Plague of London in 1665 efforts to contain the spread of the disease led to whole families being locked in their houses together if they had just one infected member. Watchmen guarded the buildings to prevent people escaping.

Worse still, families were forced by law to kill all their pets and domestic animals, in case those too became the means of spreading the dreaded infection. Nobody knew how the disease spread, and although there were lots of theories, no one guessed that rat fleas were the true culprits.

The historian reads from the Order of 1665 issued by the Lord Mayor of London and Justices of the Peace '... that no hogs, dogs, or cats, or tame pigeons, or conies, be suffered to be kept within any part of the city ...' Official exterminators were paid about two-pence for each animal they killed.

Jonah goes up and brings Pardoner down and sits with him held protectively on his lap. I reach over and stroke the cat. He seems to have grown bigger even in the short time we have had him, and a little fuzz of black hair is showing on his scarred head.

The interviewer then talks to 'local historian and poet Roger Melkin'. It is strange to see Roger on television. He talks about the plague pit, and about what a valuable member of the local history society Alice Smith is.

'I didn't know Roger was a poet,' says Jonah.

'He writes peculiar poetry that doesn't rhyme,' Mrs Bagling tells him, 'but he seems to do all right on it, except one winter when they came and cut his electricity off.'

When the news feature is over we leave Mum to talk to Mrs Bagling and we make our way upstairs. Jonah carries Pardoner, who hangs quite happily over his left shoulder, front paws dangling.

'Can I have him in my room for a while?' Jonah asks. 'You had him this morning.'

I nod and agree. I wonder if, on a day when things have started to feel just a tiny bit better, I might have lost some of my unreasonable dread of Jonah's room. Might my terror simply have come from the way I was feeling in general? I hover on the landing as Jonah turns the door handle. To my surprise Pardoner begins to struggle and tries to get down.

'Don't let him go,' I say. 'He might run downstairs and get at the poison.'

Jonah holds on tightly to the wriggling cat and goes into his room. The sound that comes out as the door swings closed behind him is not like anything I have ever heard before, not from cat nor dog nor any living creature. It is a primitive howl. It is so loud that it hurts my eardrums. I fling the door wide and see Pardoner hit the floor in a hissing, spitting frenzy. He runs downstairs so fast that his back feet overtake his front ones as he reaches the bend, and he somersaults head first into the wall. Then he rights himself, skids round the corner and is gone.

Eleven

I STAND FOR A MOMENT STARING AT JONAH'S
shocked face and lacerated arm, from which blood is
dripping on to the floorboards. I reach out a hand to him
and pat his shoulder sympathetically, then I run after the
cat. The stairs boom under my feet. I rush past Mum and
Mrs Bagling in the living room, past the poison pellets in
the kitchen. The cat flap is still swinging.

I wrench at the back door. It will not open. I try the
key but find that the door is not locked. Although the
weather is dry the door is jammed shut again as if the
wood had become swollen with damp. Then, as Mum
comes into the kitchen behind me, the door flies open
and I am through it, staring desperately up and down the
narrow alley.

Further down, where the alley curves into the courtyard, I see a flicker of black. I start to struggle along in
that direction, slipping on the moss, wrenching my ankle
on the uneven cobblestones, pushing past Roger's
dustbin which clatters and falls over as I shove it out of
my way. The obstacles and the clumsiness make the
short journey seem long, the way it is in dreams when
time isn't working properly and your normal capabilities
no longer achieve normal results.

I graze my elbow on the high wall next to me as I round
the slight curve at the end of the alley. Then I am in the
courtyard. It is empty.

In the middle, the twisted oak tree shudders in an eddy of wind. There are three ways I could go now. I could follow either of the two alleys through to Hound Hill or the main road, or I could continue on down the other narrow back alley opposite, which matches the one from which I have just emerged.

I stand still, indecisive. I am not even sure that Pardoner actually came this way. He might have gone in the opposite direction, up the hill. The flicker of black which I saw could have been anything, a blown leaf, a plastic dustbin liner. A rat.

Hidden by the curve of the alley I can hear Mum calling, 'Emily? Emily?' Her voice sounds very far away. The back doors in the opposite alley file away, green, blue, purple, black and on into greyness. Some have cat flaps in them. Might Pardoner have gone through one of these? The cat flaps are still, impenetrable. Here in the cat-deprived alleys only the wind is calling to be let in.

I walk once round the tree and then I stand still again, feeling the chill of this stone place. For reasons I don't understand, I walk round the tree again.

'Pardoner?' I call.'Pardoner?' To have had him for such a short time, and then to have lost him again, seems unbearable. Perhaps he will come home of his own accord. Suddenly, with a rush of feeling that hits me like an avalanche, I understand how the boy, Pardoner's previous owner, must feel. I sit down on the flagstones under the tree, and I know that I must find the boy again and tell him that his cat is safe.

First, though, I must find Pardoner. After that I will concentrate on finding the boy. If, as it seems, his misery has unhinged him and turned him into a burglar or even a murderer, he will obviously have to be locked up, but at least he can know his cat is all right.

The courtyard is very quiet. Mum has stopped calling

— 64 —

me now. I listen carefully for any sounds that might be a cat. Then I hum a few bars of 'Greensleeves' to break the silence, wondering a little at my choice of melody.

The smell of bread baking drifts to my nostrils. Probably Roger, I reflect, showing off his multiple domestic talents. It is a wonderful smell, nonetheless. A voice from somewhere nearby calls, 'Sarah? Sarah?' I consider how close but how separate these other people's lives are.

I have decided to take the alley through to Hound Hill, and am just about to stand up, when I hear footsteps. No, not footsteps, they are more like pushing, rustling sounds, the movement of feet in an awkward place.

For a moment I cannot tell where they are coming from because of the strange, vaultlike acoustics of this courtyard. I wait, poised to get up. Then I see that it is Roger. He is moving up and down his part of the back alley. He has not seen me. He comes down nearly as far as the courtyard and he still doesn't see me. He is scattering something from a box.

When he does see me he lets out a yelp which is rather satisfying. At least he hasn't been able to ignore my existence this time.

'Hello Roger,' I say. To my surprise he comes over and sits down next to me. I turn my head and study him, a short man in black trousers that look like school trousers, and a pressed striped shirt. 'What are you doing, Roger?' I ask him, glancing at the box in his hand. It is yellow and black and has a skull and crossbones symbol on its side.

'Poisoning vermin,' he replies. I feel a wave of alarm.

'Roger . . .' I glance up the alley to where he was scattering the contents of the box. 'Roger, if you put that stuff outside the houses, people's pets might eat it by accident.'

He shakes his head, staring at the ground and arranging some loose pebbles from under the oak tree into a straight line.

'People shouldn't let their pets out,' he says. 'Not near these busy roads. They can cause accidents, you know. They can result in people being killed. You've got to understand, Emily,' and here he stops arranging pebbles and looks me in the eye, 'how important it is to exercise responsibility, not just over pets but over everything, to stay on top of things to stay in *control*.' His voice has risen now, and become quavery. Abruptly he pauses and seems to get a grip on himself. His gaze slides away from mine. One of the pebbles is slightly out of line so he puts it exactly straight.

I feel inexpressible alarm. 'Roger, you can't always . . .'

He interrupts me. 'You see, Emily . . . well maybe you don't see because you're young and silly . . . but you will learn the importance of keeping everything in your life clean and tidy and organised. People who don't, fall victim to all sorts of terrible catastrophes. We must keep in order what we *can* keep in order, because there's so much that we cannot.'

I look at him sharply, ignoring my irritation at being called silly, and it comes to me like a flow of cold water down my spine that Roger knows something.

I search for the words to ask him what he knows, but as if feeling that he has already said too much, he gestures with his arm and changes the subject. 'There used to be a well here, in this courtyard.'

I want to stop him. I want to hurry and continue searching for Pardoner, but first it is essential that I should persuade Roger to remove the poison that he has laid, both for Pardoner's sake and for the sake of any other cats and dogs which might patrol the back alley.

'I think the well must have been in the middle, where this tree is now,' Roger is continuing. 'There's a document in the museum that says it was paved over after someone drowned themselves in it.' He taps his poison box against his palm. 'Well, I must get on.' He stands up. I stand up quickly too, knowing that questions about other matters must wait.

'Roger, look, I agree with you about pets not being let out near the main road. The thing is, though, that our kitten has escaped. I'm really worried about it and I'm afraid it might eat your poison pellets . . .' We both look round at the sound of someone else coming down the alley.

'Em! Any sign of Pardoner? Oh, hi Roger.' It is Jonah. His arm is bandaged and he looks his normal unflurried self again. He has a cigarette behind each ear and a slice of chocolate cake in his hand. It reminds me of how, when he was tiny, he never went anywhere without his comfort blanket round his neck and his teddy in his hand.

'No.' I shake my head and tell him about Roger's poison pellets. Roger looks at me with an air of hurt reproach, as if I were telling tales on him, which I am.

'Good grief! You can't do that, Rog! Don't you know it's against the law?' Jonah reels back in a parody of shock and dismay. I know from his slightly shifty look that he has just made this imaginary law up. 'Don't worry,' he continues. 'We'll help you sweep them up and we won't tell anyone, will we, Em? Then maybe you can help us look for our cat.'

Roger splutters and protests but Jonah continues, 'Our rat catcher is here again. He's left his baseball bat at home but he's got something that looks like a guided missile launcher this time. We're getting it all done for nothing, apparently, because the council's in a panic about there being plague in the street. You could ask him to do your place as well, Roger.'

Roger stares at Jonah with an expression of suspicion and hostility, but then reluctantly agrees. 'I wouldn't want to harm anyone's pet,' he says grudgingly.

As we are helping him sweep up the pellets the rat catcher appears in the alley. He is wearing khaki trousers, a camouflage pattern shirt and combat boots. Over everything is a rustling see-through plastic cover-all, with big rubber gloves on his hands and a transparent protective helmet on his head. He looks like a cross between Action Man and an astronaut.

He nods to the three of us, then stares disapprovingly at some items of rubbish which must have fallen out of Roger's bin when I knocked it over, teabags and cabbage stalks and an economy baked beans tin.

'This won't do, you know,' he snaps through his plastic mouthpiece. 'If you leave rubbish lying around it's no wonder you get rats. It's a godsend to rats is this alley.' A bluebottle buzzes past his ear like a small Flymo and he bats it out of the sky and stamps it underfoot. Then he unslings something that looks like a large, hollow drill from his shoulder. 'I'm here to block up possible rat entry holes with this quick drying cement and put filters over all the drains. Contract from the council.'

He sets about his work. 'Do you know that rats sometimes come up out of lavatories?' he adds con-versationally over his shoulder. 'Swim the U-bend, they do. Best to put a heavy brick on the lid overnight.'

I look at Roger's glassy expression of horror as I hand him his broom. I want to say 'There there Roger, it's all right,' but I decide that forgiveness and reconciliation can wait for another day. 'We'd better look for the cat now,' I say as kindly as I can, realising that from Roger's point of view, rats exploding out of lavatories must surely represent the ultimate in things being out of control.

I look round at the cobblestones. It hasn't been easy brushing between them. 'Is that all of it?' I ask. Everyone peers closely and the poison does all seem to be gone. I thank Roger for letting us clear it up, and apologise for the waste, then I quickly turn back towards the courtyard. I am in a hurry now. We have lost too much time.

'I'll help you,' says Roger. 'I'll help you look for your cat.'

I turn back to him in surprise. 'Thank you, Roger.'

The rat catcher stops scraping at the walls looking for holes and turns round too.

'Lost yer cat? What does it look like?'

I tell him.

'I'll keep an eye open for it too.' He nods at me. 'Got a soft spot for cats, I have. Cats and me, we understand each other I reckon. We're in the same line of business, you could say.'

I thank him too, and Roger, Jonah and I split up to search for Pardoner along the streets and alleys. Later Mum and Mrs Bagling come out and join us. As the late afternoon turns to evening and we keep returning home from unsuccessful searching to see if anyone else has had any luck, the rat catcher brings us several of the neighbourhood cats to inspect, a long-haired tabby, a Siamese, a ginger tom.

'No,' explains Mum gently. She seems to be feeling a little more patient with him now, and she describes Pardoner yet again.

The evening grows warm as the wind drops and a late sun comes out, dipping towards the horizon like a red balloon. At seven o'clock it starts to grow dark and we realise that for now we have to give up. An intense sadness overwhelms me.

Mrs Bagling invites us all into her house for sherry. She has been wearing a fur coat, high heels, powder, lipstick and plenty of mascara as she trails the streets calling 'Pussy! Pussy!' Now her mascara is running into the folds of her cheeks and she looks exhausted.

'We've done our best,' says Mum, looking very upset. 'Thank you all very much.'

The rat catcher flops down into one of Mrs Bagling's pink velvet chairs. 'It seems as if everybody's been out looking for their blessed cats today,' he says. He stretches out his legs and downs his sherry in one mouthful. 'There was some hippy layabout up the hill saying he'd lost his cat. Too drunk to talk clear, he was. Dearie me, young folks these days . . .'

'Hippy layabout . . . ?' I ask swiftly. The rat catcher and Roger are ignoring me and talking to each other. I stand up. 'Excuse me, did you say hippy layabout? Somebody in a peculiar coat and boots, who was looking for his cat?'

They are laughing together at a joke and don't even hear me.

'*Excuse me* . . .' I want to shake the rat catcher, but instead I just grab him by the lapels. 'Where did you see this hippy layabout?' I shout into his face.

'What . . . eh? Oh, up the hill . . . somewhere near the DSS office, needless to say. Between the museum and the antique shop . . . is he a friend of yours? You want to watch out having friends of that sort . . .'

'Emily!' Mum sounds appalled as she detaches me from the rat catcher.

'Sorry Mum. I have to go. I'm sorry, I'm just going to search a bit more. Sorry,' I call back to the rat catcher. 'Goodbye Mrs Bagling. Thank you for the sherry.' Then I am out through the door and running up Hound Hill.

Twelve

*T*HIS IS STRANGE GROUND. I HAVE NEVER HAD reason to come this way before. I am breathless by the time I reach the top of the hill.

There is no one else about. This is the first odd thing that strikes me as I puff to a halt next to a group of small shops. Surely people should be coming home from work or going out to the pub at this time of an evening. The wide blue twilight is empty of people but full of the raucous calling of rooks that circle from a copse of trees behind the shops.

The second odd thing I notice is that the street lights have not yet come on, even though dimness is already creeping out of the alleys and settling on the streets.

On the opposite side of the road is a flat-fronted building with elegant fanlight windows. A sign in its front garden says HOUND HILL LOCAL HISTORY MUSEUM. Next to it a block of offices is labelled DEPARTMENT OF SOCIAL SECURITY. This must be the place where the rat catcher saw his so called hippy layabout. How many young men with eccentric clothes and incomprehensible speech are likely to be looking for their cats round here at the same time? It *must* have been Pardoner's owner.

I stand still under the rooky light and wait. Of course, he might well have moved on to search elsewhere.

Perhaps, frustratingly, he will always be one step ahead of me.

Yet in some strange way I actually feel as if he is close. Maybe I really am going mad. Maybe that knock on the head was just the last straw for my poor brain. It is as if he is behind a wall, round a corner, beyond the trees where the rooks nest, near enough to sense but far enough to hide.

I have the same feeling that I used to have when I played hide-and-seek with Jonah and our cousins in Great Grandmother Strachan's vast wild garden, a feeling of someone lurking unseen, watching silently close by.

I move to stand in the doorway of one of the shops. Ridiculously, I want my back protected. I don't want anyone to be able to creep up behind me. The rooks are making such a noise that I would not be able to hear someone coming. This is the doorway of an antique shop. I glance in the windows on either side of me. A carved wooden trunk on legs is labelled 'Restoration coffer'. In the opposite window a massive dark chest with an iron lock is inscribed with the date 1587 and labelled 'Elizabethan dower chest'.

I wonder if Mum knows about this shop. She can no longer afford antiques, but she still enjoys looking. I peer over the top of a pile of rubbish waiting to be collected, to see the interior of the shop. It extends a long way back and is crowded with beautiful furniture and ornaments.

I think of Roger, and the sudden feeling I had that he knew something — something about the strangeness of this place. Maybe I was wrong. Maybe Roger is just naturally strange.

Soon it will be dark. The street lights still have not come on. There must be an electricity failure. I might as well search a little more for Pardoner while the light lasts, since the boy is clearly not here.

'Pardoner?' I walk along the row of shops, a butcher's, a fishmonger's, a newsagent, a shop that sells fancy candles, and back to the antique shop to stand in the doorway again. 'Pardoner?'

'Pardoner?' The voice makes me jump with fright. It is right behind me, at shoulder level. It is rough and rasping as if one of the rooks had spoken. I jerk round with a cry.

'Oh . . .'

How could I have missed him? How could I not have seen him in this doorway? The pile of rubbish that I scarcely noticed is not rags and boxes at all. It is a beggar, and now it has risen to its feet.

I have seen beggars before. You can't avoid it in London, can you, but I have never seen anyone like this. He is stooped, and draped only in a few filthy rags. He is so thin that the bones of his skeleton show through his skin. Behind a clotted beard his face looks like pewter, grey and shiny, bloated into hardness. He stinks of something worse than anything I have ever smelt.

'You require pardon, mistress? I can grant you pardon for your sins, if you will grant me a farthing for some food.' His speech is painfully forced out through cracked and bleeding lips. He is even more difficult to understand than the boy was.

'I . . . I have come out without any money. I'm so sorry . . .'

I can see that he does not understand me. He holds out his hands, cupped, under my nose, the fingertips swollen and purple, like plums. On his bare chest and arms are dark blotches, from deep red through to black, flamed red at the edges.

'Help me, lady!' he wails, and raises his eyes and his hands to the darkening sky. As he emerges from the doorway, teetering bow-legged, the wind ripples his rags like bunting, and I see in the hollows under his arms the beginnings of strange swellings. He holds his arms out from them as if they were impeding his movement.

Suddenly he grabs at me. 'Alms! Alms for pity's sake . . .' He seems out of his senses. It is almost dark. I feel afraid of him but driven to try and help him.

'Look, there's a hostel at the bottom of the hill, beyond the park. I saw it the other day. A Salvation Army hostel. Go down there. They'll help you.'

Suddenly his attention is distracted, and so is mine. I take the opportunity to step back from him a little and stare across the road to where there is a commotion going on. Outside the DSS offices people are shouting and throwing things. I am so relieved to see other people that I really couldn't care less if they are rioting.

It is hard to see properly. In the last of the day's light I move to stand in the middle of the road, and peer at them. Then I see that they too are beggars. They too are as poor and distressed as this man who has now sidled up close to me again. He has started laughing and chuckling in a mad undertone.

Abruptly one of the crowd, a young man with a gaunt and black-stubbled face, takes a pace back, then runs and hurls a brick through the window of the DSS offices. The glass explodes with a crash and flies all over the road. Surely someone must hear it. Surely the police must come. A pathetic, thin cheer goes up from the vagrants and two of the younger ones briefly hold hands and dance round in a circle.

'Ring-a-ring-a-roses . . .' The beggar next to me mutters it in a tuneless whisper, and because he is so close I can see that tears are spurting from his eyes. 'Pocket full of posies. You got posies, lady? You got pockets?' He thrusts his disfigured chest at me and shouts, 'All fall down! All fall down!'

Suddenly the beggars see me. They fall silent. Then they start to advance towards me. A titter goes up from the younger ones as they spread out to encircle me. I back away but there is nowhere to go because the antique shop is behind me and the beggar is dodging from side to side in front of me.

One of them, a woman with wedge cheekbones and a sunken, lipless mouth, calls out, 'Leave her alone, Matchlock! I'll warrant she does not have the distemper yet. You'll infect her, you old fool. Get back. She's done no harm to you.'

The beggar whom she has addressed as Matchlock is now so close to me that I can feel the unnatural feverish heat coming off his body. He reaches out a bone-fingered hand to take hold of my wrist. I cringe away. I dare not push him. He looks almost as if he might drop apart.

'Aye, get off her, Matchlock,' calls the gaunt young man who threw the brick. 'Let her be. She's afeared. She's crazed with fear. Just look at her.'

'Look at her clothes!' cries another. 'Maybe it's a lad — it's wearing breeches.'

The woman pushes forward and stares at me, hands on hips, still keeping her distance from Matchlock. 'Maybe she's been thrown out. Maybe she wants to join us.' There is a questioning note in her voice.

The others are all shouting at me now.

'What are you doing out on Beggarsgate at night, lass?'

'Are you off to a masque, dressed so?'

'Nay, cannot be a masque — they're forbidden for fear of contagion.'

'Are you wanting to join us?' the woman repeats. 'Have you been driven out? You'd be best off with us. We don't have the contagion yet. We're beggars now but we were all household servants before, whose masters and mistresses laid us off and fled to the country to escape the pestilence. We protect each other from the likes of Matchlock. For him it is too late.'

'Driven out . . .' whimpers Matchlock next to me. 'Aye, driven out . . .' He gives a sudden wild laugh. 'But we allus come back, don't we. Aye, we allus come back. We're like the rats. We allus come back.'

That is when a terrible suspicion starts to grow in my mind, and as it does, I hear, once more in the distance, the clanging of a bell.

Thirteen

'**D**EAD CART'S COMING.'

Matchlock says it without emphasis. 'Dead cart's coming,' he repeats. 'Oh, some's dead and some's dead drunk and some's dead proud and fancy and there's not much difference once they're all tipped into the pit together. Come on, let's put her in the dead cart, for she's so proud and fancy in her boy's breeches and no good to anybody.'

Seeing my opportunity, as he cackles at his own wit, I try to dodge past the beggar, but he lunges at me, howling with laughter now. 'I'll be on the dead cart meself soon. Teee heee . . .' His voice has risen to a banshee wail. 'Oh we'll all sleep tight down in hell tonight . . .'

The other beggars are whispering among themselves while I try to evade Matchlock's disease-embossed arms. The others are clearly afraid to come close enough to help me. In desperation I push at Matchlock's clawlike hands and try to edge round him.

The bell is drawing closer, and now I can see a flickering light, far off down the hill.

'I can see the linksman's light,' says the woman beggar. 'We'd better move. The pestilence is all over them.' She looks again at me. 'Come with us. Come on. Just run.' She comes up behind Matchlock and claps her hands. As he jerks round with a shout, I dodge past him

— 77 —

and out into the middle of the road. Now I can see what is coming.

Trudging up the hill at the front of the small procession is a man carrying a flaming torch in front of him. Next to him walks another man, younger but ill-looking, swinging a handbell slowly at his side. Sometimes it rings and sometimes it doesn't. Behind them two horses pull a rough wooden cart that bounces and rattles over the cobbles. The driver is slumped in his seat, his head on his chest.

Untidily in the back, jerking with the movement of the cart, is a jumble of white-wrapped bundles. From one, I see a hand protruding, moving up and down as if waving when the cart hits bumps. As it draws nearer I see feet and legs and faces, discoloured and distended, their wrappings falling loose, as if applied with the carelessness of despair.

The two horses exude heat and steaming breath and the smells of hay and warm stables. Their heavy slow feet clack on the cobbles. Cobbles — I look down and it hardly comes as any surprise to me to find that the street is now cobbled, where before there had been tarmac.

The driver raises his head and shouts something. For a moment we all stand and listen, as if turned to stone by this picture from hell.

'Bring out your dead!' he calls in a hoarse voice. 'Bring out your dead!'

Behind the cart, filthy and tired looking, staggering along as if drunk, comes another man. He carries before him a long red stick, sometimes leaning on it for support.

I realise with a start that Matchlock is back by my side. Here in the open, I fear him less. He is almost too pitiful to fear. He points to the man with the red stick. 'I worked as a bearer like him, shifting the dead, afore I was taken too ill, lady,' he whispers. 'Once upon a time I

—— 78 ——

could have throwed you on that there cart . . .' His suffocating smell and raging heat make me feel dizzy. I move carefully away from him and towards the beggar woman, who has fallen behind her companions to wait for me.

As I do so, another voice comes from the direction of the antique shop.

'Come over here!'

I strain to see into the shadows. None of the shops has lights on in the windows. I must go to one side of the road or the other, because the dead cart is coming up the middle.

'Quickly! Get away from that beggar and come over here!'

The advancing torch light now shows a figure running towards me, a figure I know. Matchlock reaches out as if to grab me, but Pardoner's owner grabs me first and pulls me away to the side of the road, into the antique shop doorway.

'Are you mad?' he enquires politely. 'Standing there waiting to be run down?'

His long dark hair is loose and his coat is trailing half on and half off, revealing a frilly shirt. He looks as if he has just woken up. It is clear from his self-possessed attitude, though, that this is the boy as he was when I first met him on my back doorstep, and not the crazed and despairing burglar who droned on about not being allowed out. I am at a loss to understand the difference, and why there appear to be two versions of him. I am at a loss to understand any of this.

He is looking at me. I consider his question.

'Possibly,' I reply.

Matchlock is now rolling in the gutter nearby, dribbling and weeping.

'May God have mercy on you,' whispers Pardoner's

owner. He takes my hand and pulls me away towards the candle shop. There is a light in its doorway now. A large candle is billowing out greasy, foul-smelling smoke. In the middle of the road the dead cart goes by, the linksman's flame roaring high and brassy, dripping hot tar on to the road ahead of him and throwing false movement on to the faces of the dead.

In this light the houses look different, the windows smaller, the doors lower and rougher. On the door of the house next to the candle shop is a large cross half a metre high, painted in dark red. There are some words below it. I pause just long enough to read them. 'May the Lord have mercy upon us'.

The other beggars have left now, spilling down the hill, pouring down Beggarsgate and out of sight. Outside the house with the cross on its door stands a burly man with a sharpened wooden stick. He looks like a bouncer.

'Good night, watchman,' says Pardoner's owner.

'Good night, sir,' says the watchman.

The smell of the candle grows worse as we draw nearer to it. I turn to the young man.

'Thank you for helping me. I don't know what I should have done. I . . . I think I must be as mad as that beggar though because, I really don't understand . . .'

He stops, and stares at me silently for a moment.

'Nor I,' he says at last.

I look back to where Matchlock is now limping and stumbling after the other beggars, trying to catch them up.

'Can't we . . . help him?'

'How? There is no cure for plague, as well you know, despite all the false and expensive treatments that the quack physicians sell. Two months ago he would have been put in a pest-house, but now that they are all full and mostly untended . . .'

With his words, he confirms the impossible and grotesque suspicion that has grown in my mind. Plague. Matchlock has plague. His symptoms are those I heard earlier described on the television news.

'What about antibiotics . . . ?' I know how foolish this is as soon as I have said it, for whatever is happening, whether or not I am mad, antibiotics are as remote from Matchlock as they are from a poverty stricken Indian villager dying fifty miles from the nearest international aid unit.

'What . . . what is your name?' I ask the boy.

'Seth,' he replies, letting go of my hand and turning to face me. 'What is yours?'

I am about to reply, but there comes a distant shout from somewhere down the hill.

'Emily? Emily?'

I turn towards it. It is Roger's voice.

'Yes?' I shout.

'Emily!' Mum's voice joins Roger's. The smell of the candle intensifies suddenly and I am enveloped in a stinking cloud of smoke as a gust of wind buffets out the flame. In the darkness I stare about me foolishly.

'Seth? Where are you? Seth!'

'Emily.' It is Roger reaching the top of the hill, his weak electric torch beam wavering as he breaks into a trot. 'Better come home now, Emily. It's dark. You won't find your cat tonight.'

A few moments later Mum joins him. She is also carrying an electric torch. These seem somehow less real than the linksman's flaming beacon. Roger takes hold of Mum's hand.

'Come on, Em,' says Mum. 'We'll search some more tomorrow, before you and Jonah go off to visit Dad.'

Incomprehensibly, she does not extract her hand from Roger's, nor does she beat his brains to a pulp with her torch. From the depths of coldness I ask, 'Did you see the beggars?'

Abruptly Roger shines his torch into my face. I push it away.

'Beggars?' asks Mum.

'Look!' I gesture towards the hill, the candle shop, the watchman, the house with the cross on its door, but they have all gone. The candle shop is closed and unlit. The greasy smoke has cleared. Seth is no longer there in his frilly shirt and wild hair.

'The rat catcher said the power failure might have been caused by the rats gnawing through the cables,' says Mum, turning to lead the way back down the hill. 'So I can't say I noticed any beggars in this dim light.'

'Wait.' I whisper it, then I borrow Mum's torch and make my way across the road. Half way across I pause. The tarmac is sticky underfoot. I look down. There is a shiny patch, a small dripped puddle of melted tar where I am walking, where the linksman walked with his burning beacon.

Roger is following me. Unsteadily I move on, to the far side of the road. I shine the torch towards the DSS offices, moving the beam to and fro across the rows of windows.

'What? What is it?' asks Roger in a strained voice, his own torch beam following mine.

At first I think there is nothing, but then I see it. It is not the gaping hole with fallen glass that I had been looking for. Instead it is a small, star-shaped crack from which just one shard hangs loose.

I look at Roger and he looks back at me, and I see that the hand with which he holds his torch is shaking.

Fourteen

'I'M GLAD YOU'RE HERE, EMILY,' SAYS ROGER. 'I can't tell you how glad I am to have someone so close who can also see them.'

It is the following morning. We are sitting in the living room. I stare at him.

'Who *are* they, Roger? *What* . . . are they?'

He shakes his head. 'They're the beggars of Beggarsgate. That's all I know. The past is alive in this street, Emily. The past is . . . the past is present. I think it just somehow never went away properly. It has stayed on in the stones and earth and the air that we breathe, and in some mysterious way some of us can glimpse it. It's as if it's there round every corner all the time. I think for a few rare people it's even possible to stumble right back into it, and for short periods of time lose all contact with the present day.'

I wonder, with a sudden chill, if this is what happened to me last night, or nearly happened perhaps, since the shops and the DSS office and other elements of the present day were still there. I saw the past last night, but how close did I come to falling right into it? The street lamps were there, but they did not contain the power to shine. The beggars and the dead cart were there, but they did not contain the power to keep me. What about next time? I find that I am shivering.

It is still early in the morning. A bright beam of

sunlight is shining in through the window, angled like a support beam from the window to my feet. In it hang tiny dust motes. I stare at the dust. It was once dogs, cats and furniture. It was once cavemen and Roman soldiers, buried treasure and dinosaurs and the volcanoes that made the earth the shape it is now. I rub my eyes and push my fingers through my hair and dust motes fly off me along the line of light, curling and spiralling in on themselves. Tiny fragments of my hair and skin go off into history, to join everything else that ever passed this way, animal and human, joy, pain, and plague.

'Do you know a young man called Seth?' I ask Roger.

'Seth?'

'A tall boy with dark hair. I think he lived above the bakery, possibly on the site where this house stands now.' On my lips are the words 'and he may be the local murderer' but after last night, with Seth's seeming return to self-control, I can no longer believe it of him, so the words remain unspoken.

'Oh yes, Seth. I've heard of him but I haven't seen him. I just see the beggars as a group, and sometimes a few other shadowy figures in the background . . .'

'Emily! Jonah!' Mum comes round the bend of the stairs with her hands full of pieces of cardboard cut from the insides of cereal boxes. On each she has written in large red lettering 'MISSING — YOUNG BLACK CAT WITH SCARRED HEAD AND BENT TAIL' followed by our telephone number. 'There's just time to put these in shop windows and tack a few on to trees before I drive you over to Dad's,' she continues.

Roger gets up from the sofa and takes them from her. The extraordinary conversation we have just had hangs between us like a genie unexpectedly released from a bottle. We cannot look directly at each other.

'I have worried about that cat all night,' says Mum,

looking round for her bag. Roger shuffles the pieces of cardboard in his hands and stares down at them. I notice his hands, short and square with very neat fingernails.

'Cats are very self-sufficient, you know,' he says in a useless attempt at normality. His eyes flick up to mine and down again. We follow Mum to the door.

It is a very bright, still day today. The wind has dropped completely. A late swallow circles the chimneys and is gone, heading south across other skies and continents and time zones. I walk next to Roger.

'I smelt the tallow candle and I knew then,' he says under his breath. 'Even before you said anything. They stink, those tallow candles. They were made from animal fat, you know. Sometimes they even had bits of animal flesh left in them. The poor had tallow candles. The rich had beeswax.'

I look sideways at him. Mum and Jonah are walking behind us. I can hear Mum saying, '. . . and I'm sure it was rat droppings I found in the larder this morning, and one of these cereal boxes I've been cutting up had been chewed . . .'

Next to me, Roger is taking small, precise steps, placing his feet neatly in the middle of the paving stones and never stepping on a line. He glances at me as if to check that he still has my attention.

'It was the law, you see,' he continues, 'that every householder on or near a street had to display a lighted candle in their front window during the dark evenings. If they forgot, they were fined a shilling, which was an awful lot of money in those days. It was part of Charles II's attempts to clean up London and make it safer. The stench in a poor area like Beggarsgate must have been enough to knock you off your feet.'

'I suppose they would have become used to it though.'

'Yes, and I daresay there were worse smells all over the

place that we wouldn't put up with now.'

'Mm.' I think of Matchlock's vile odour, and even of comparatively sweet-smelling Seth's faint charity shop fragrance.

'Of course, during times of plague, an unlighted window could mean the worst, not just that someone had forgotten.'

I think of all the unlighted windows in Beggarsgate last night, and I feel a terrible sense of disquietude. I think of Matchlock and his sores and swellings. How many others in equal agony lie behind those darkened windows of Beggarsgate, hearing the dead cart go by? How long can Matchlock survive with no one to help him, roaming the streets crazed and exploding with putrefaction? I do not yet know, on that sunny September morning, how much worse people can still become.

'Perhaps you would like to come to the museum with me, Emily,' Roger says hesitantly. 'It tells you all about Hound Hill there. You should . . .' Here he pauses again, and it occurs to me that perhaps he is afraid of me. I feel slightly ashamed. 'You should possibly join the Hound Hill Local History Society.'

Local history, how ridiculous it sounds. What on earth can a local history society have to say to me that I can't just go off and experience for myself, the way things are going? It will be a crowd of silly people like Roger, dedicated to building silly fences round artefacts such as the plague stone. I think of the plague stone. Perhaps, after all, I should join.

I glance at Roger. 'I might.' We walk on up the hill in silence for a few moments.

'But what *are* those people, Roger?' I say as the shops at the top of the hill come into sight. 'They're not ghosts. They're solid. They speak to me. They touch me. They *break windows*. And what about the cat? It belongs to Seth, and he's one of them. It's a real cat, Roger. It slurps its milk and moults all over the furniture.'

Roger shakes his head, leafing through the notices in his hand and putting them all the same way up. Then he arranges them into size order.

'This has all been very bad for my nerves,' he mutters. 'I'd move away, but somehow once you're here, you stay. And stay and stay . . . Like the past has somehow stayed, Emily. Not the romantic past but the real past when people starved in gutters and were superstitious and saw ghosts and died of diseases we have eliminated now. I'm afraid I don't know what those people are. Perhaps they are a phenomenon that doesn't have a name.'

We reach the top of the hill. Mum shares out the notices and we take them into the shops and ask for them to be displayed in windows. The shops are all open and busy. It is Saturday morning. I go into the candle shop. It is full of sweet-smelling candles in bright colours, candles in different shapes and sizes, garden candles in plantpots, floating candles, beeswax candles in red, green and amber, but there are no tallow candles. There is nothing evil-smelling here today.

When we have finished we cross the road to where a workman is nailing a piece of chipboard over the cracked window of the DSS office. Mum asks him to fix one of her notices to it and he agrees.

The museum is open and we go in.

'Poor Alice,' says Roger. 'They say she'll be all right though. She's on tetracycline. Of course they didn't have antibiotics during the Great Plague of London. Might have been a whole different story if they had. I think they're treating your teacher as a precaution too, Emily, Miss Patel.'

'Really?'

Mum and Jonah move away to look at a display of watchmen's lanterns in a glass case, and suddenly a horrible thought strikes me. I sit down on one of the upholstered benches.

'Roger?'

He sits down next to me.

'Roger, how closely have you seen the beggars? Do you know that at least one of them has plague?'

He looks dismayed. 'No, really? I knew they were from a time when plague was around, but I can't see them that closely. It's just, sort of, an impression I get, of people, you know, shambling along the street. It's like a very old film, one of those silent movies actually, because I can't hear them either. That's what is so frightening, the fact that they're so obviously not really there. Sometimes I can smell them though . . .' He shudders violently. 'Oh, I dread that. I can sometimes even smell those tallow candles inside my own house.'

I shift away from him, feeling sick with fright.

'You see Roger . . . I think they might be from the time of the Great Plague; and to me they do seem like real people. They seem to be really there. They seem so real that . . .' I can't say it. The sickness and headache that I haven't felt for a couple of days sweep back over me. I feel very hot and tired and I want to go home. I stand up and walk towards the door. Roger follows me and takes hold of my arm. I shake him loose and face him and tell him about Matchlock, with his blotches and swellings.

'I can't remember if he actually managed to touch me,' I babble. I find that I am nearly in tears. 'But, you see, I might be infectious myself now . . .'

To my surprise Roger puts his arm around me. I see Mum watching us with a very surprised and pleased expression. Roger gives my shoulders a little shake and peers into my face.

'Emily, what you say is very interesting, but these people aren't really real. What we're seeing must be almost certainly due to some strange freak of time. Someone who had the plague more than three hundred years ago couldn't possibly infect you now. It could be the terrible anguish of that time that has somehow printed this piece of history on our street.'

Mum comes up and smiles at us. 'Jonah and I are just going to pin some notices to the trees on the hill,' she says. 'Do you two want to stay and look round here a bit longer? I'm going to go and have another look at that Restoration coffer afterwards. It's one of the most beautiful pieces of furniture I've ever seen. Broke or not, I'm tempted to buy it. It would look wonderful under the window in the living room.'

For some reason I want to say to her, 'Don't, Mum! Don't bring any more of the past into our house.' But that would be ridiculous. Roger smiles and nods and watches her go, folding up one of the pieces of cardboard very small without seeming to notice what he is doing.

'Roger . . .' Gently I take it from him before he can ruin it completely. He looks at it in my hand and shrugs and shakes his head.

'They're a waste of time.' He gestures at the notice. 'A complete waste of time.' It's no good putting up notices for a cat over three hundred years old. That cat is not where any of us can find it.'

He crosses to the reception desk where an elderly woman is fitting leaflets into a rack.

'Hello Roger. How are you? Are you coming tonight?'

'Hello Evelyn. I'm fine, thanks.' They exchange a few words and Roger picks up a leaflet and brings it over to me. It has a picture of an ancient helmet on the front and

— 89 —

the words 'Hound Hill Local History Society'. Roger hands it to me. 'You should join us, Emily. There's a meeting tonight.'

His words have a strange intensity.

'I might not be back from Dad's in time.'

'Try. I think you need us, Emily. I think we need you even more.'

Fifteen

WHEN WE ARRIVE BACK HOME MUM FINDS THAT her car won't start, so while she and Roger stand with the bonnet up, staring despairingly and uncomprehendingly at the engine, Jonah and I set off to cross London by Tube. I am quite glad. For some reason, I don't want to be shut up in a car just now.

We change at Oxford Circus and Victoria. Everywhere there are beggars. These are polite beggars, old women, young mothers with lethargic children, strong young men with desperate faces, teenagers younger than Jonah and me.

'Spare any change?' they ask humbly, suppressing what must surely be an urge to say to these well-dressed Saturday shoppers, 'Give us a tenner. You can afford it.' Some have labelled themselves with bits of cardboard that look like our lost cat notices. 'Homeless and hungry', their notices say. These beggars don't menace, mock or encircle us. They are not angry enough, not yet. I give them fivepences. It is all I can afford. Jonah gives them nothing. He has used up his week's allowance already. We spend the entire journey discussing ways in which he could try to give up smoking.

Dad looks just as he always does, confident and jolly, when he meets us at Norwood Junction Station. I suppose, looking at him objectively, that he is quite handsome. He has acquired a tan since we last saw him. I rush up to him and hug him.

'How was the holiday, Dad?' Jonah asks as he and Dad shake hands. This is relatively new, this handshaking. Dad decided a few months ago that Jonah was now too grown up for hugs. Personally I think his timing was seriously off, what with the move and everything. Jonah only started smoking when he stopped getting hugs.

'Oh, great, thanks Jonah. Provence is *so* hot at this time of year.' We all get into the car. I reflect rather resentfully that Dad's car has no trouble in starting.

'Strapped in?' asks Dad, an old habit that is rather endearing. 'Now children, you both remember my mentioning Carmel? Well, I have something to tell you . . .'

The visit is a disaster. Dad's flat, on the first floor of a large house set back from the road, is full of scents of fresh coffee and garlic when we arrive. Carmel meets us on the step, managing to look both glamorous and wholesome at the same time. She is tall and slim with long shiny brown hair and large white teeth. She is overwhelmingly friendly, but I still feel as if she would like to bite us with her big white teeth.

Dad's flat is full of Carmel's things. She has filled the living room and bedroom with fragrant flowers, and the bathroom with expensive lotions and bath oils. Together with the coffee and garlic smells they comprise a dizzying cocktail of aroma. I feel suffocated, as if my nostrils were plugged with bath oil and cloves of garlic.

'Smells like a flyspray factory,' mutters Jonah, not quietly enough.

We play about with the meal of mussels in cream sauce, tossed green salad and hot Greek bread which Carmel has prepared. I try to force some of it down while

Dad and Carmel make stilted conversation. They tell us about their holiday and ask us about school and the new house.

Suppose I just say it's haunted? Suppose I say that the Great Plague of London still lives on in Hound Hill, both in the past in a streetful of phantom beggars and in the present in the person of Alice Smith who brought it back from India, almost as if the street had called it. Not to mention one of my teachers who is being treated with antibiotics just in case. Oh don't worry about us, Dad. You just abandoned us to poverty and a potentially fatal disease. Nothing serious.

Of course, I don't say any of this. It becomes obvious anyway that Jonah has decided to be rude. At lunch he rocks to and fro on the back legs of his chair, one of the old household crimes-of-crimes that we somehow seem to have stopped worrying about at Hound Hill. After lunch he sits in a corner and plays with Andromeda the cat and ignores Carmel.

Carmel tells us how wonderfully Dad's business is doing and Dad says, 'Oh heavens, it's not that great,' and Carmel gives him a playful slap and says, 'He's so modest, silly boy,' and Jonah makes a vomiting face behind their backs.

Later we go shopping with Dad and come back laden with bribery in the form of t-shirts and CDs from Our Price. Jonah plays his Walkman very loudly in the car on the way back and pretends not to hear remarks addressed to him.

'I want you both to like Carmel,' says Dad rather pathetically. 'Do you like her?'

Jonah, who is sitting in the front, hums in tune with the crashing of Heavy Metal music coming out of his earphones. Clearly it is up to me.

'We don't know her yet, Dad,' I reply. 'I expect we'll

get used to her. You . . . could have warned us though.'

Dad is about to answer me, and I am touched by how vulnerable his face looks in the rear view mirror, but Jonah turns his music up and Dad snaps at him instead and tells him that he's probably destroying his eardrums.

Over tea of scones, butter and home made quince jam Jonah mentions, as if by accident, Mum's growing friendship with Roger. Dad gives him a very startled look indeed.

'Our parents are hopeless,' says Jonah on the way back across London. 'I shall never be like that, messing up one marriage, then risking it all over again.'

I nod in agreement. I have changed two pounds of the money Dad gave me into tenpences and I give these out, one by one, to the beggars. I feel despairing at how little difference it will make. I feel guilty at having a comfortable home, and at mentally having applied the word poverty to it.

Jonah also has some change now, and when he has used it all up, he gives an old man at Oxford Circus his last cigarettes.

We get off the train at Blacksmith's Corner Station and walk up past the church and park, back to Hound Hill. It is a relief to be back . . . I almost said home. I almost said it is a relief to be back home, and I meant the house on Hound Hill. What on earth am I talking about? What is happening to me? This is not home. Hound Hill or Beggarsgate, it will never be home.

Mum and Roger are sitting on the sofa watching the news and eating popcorn. They smile, and Mum nods with her mouth full in the direction of the teapot and the popcorn bowl. 'Help yourselves,' she says indistinctly.

Roger looks as if he owns the place. I am relieved to

find that I can still manage a flurry of hatred for him. At least I haven't gone completely soft in the head.

'Mum, do you know that Dad's got a woman living with him?' asks Jonah tightly.

Mum looks away from the television and regards us both for a moment. 'Carmel? Yes, I know. Was she there? Oh, I'm sorry. I should have warned you.'

'Is that the one you call The Camel?' enquires Roger and they both collapse in fits of giggles. I am outraged. It's nauseating. How can Mum treat this disintegrating family as a joke? And how dare *Roger* laugh at Dad?

They are talking about the Indian plague on the television.

' . . . bubonic plague, characterised by swellings in the armpits, neck and groin has an incubation period of up to ten days. It is spread by the bites of rodent fleas which attack human beings once all their normal rodent hosts are dead. However the epidemic now seems to be reaching a second stage where a complication occurs, and the illness manifests itself as the even more dangerous pneumonic plague which can kill in three to four days.

'In its pneumonic state the infection causes the lungs to fill with fluid and is spread by breath droplets directly from sufferer to sufferer. Victims experience severe breathing difficulties, choking and vomiting. A further even more serious state, septicaemic plague, can occur when the bacillus invades the patient's bloodstream to such an extent that brain damage and death may occur within twenty-four hours, and before any other signs of plague have had time to appear . . .'

Roger is looking at me.

'Are you coming to the meeting?' he asks.

I hesitate, then nod. He stands up and reaches for his jacket. 'Time to go then.'

Sixteen

IT IS A GREY EVENING. LOW CLOUDS OVER THE chimneys hint at mist or drizzle later. Roger and I walk in silence. I want to ask him more about the local history society but I am too annoyed with him.

At first all I see is a flutter of black at the corner of my eye. Something on the other side of the road. I barely glance round. Then there is a movement in the alley we are just passing, on my left. I turn sharply. I can see nothing there. I was mistaken. It must have been a flurry of dust in the wind.

But there is no wind. I slow my step and look from side to side. Nothing. I glance at Roger. He too is slowing down, but he is just smiling at me patiently as if he thinks I am tired.

'All right, Emily?'

There are dark shapes in the gutter further up the hill. Suddenly I don't want to go up there. I hear something shuffle close behind me, but when I whip round, there's nothing.

'Roger . . .' I stand still. He stops too. His face changes.

'Emily, what can you see?'

A car goes by. I wait for its sound to die away. A young couple walk in the opposite direction on the other side of the road. A boy whizzes down the hill on his bike. A man with a Sainsbury's bag trudges up behind us and goes into one of the houses. I can hear nothing and see nothing that is out of the ordinary.

I shake my head and take a few more steps. I keep looking all round, at the near gutter and the far gutter. There is just the usual rubbish, squashed drinks cans, bits of old newspaper. I look behind me. The street stretches away down the hill towards the park.

Roger is frowning now. He keeps looking at me. A helicopter goes overhead. I am unnerved by the noise and what it may be masking. As it fades I hear a violent scrabbling in the next alley.

'Listen!' I put my hand on Roger's arm. 'Did you hear that?'

He shakes his head. 'What?'

We reach the alley and I peer down it. The street lamps are working tonight, making long shadows on the pavements. Something moves in the alley between the houses. I stand very still and stare into the narrow place between the two walls. Something touches my ankle. I shriek and jump back, and I see it go. A rat. A big black rat with a snaking tail and large ears is rushing along the edge of the pavement.

I can't speak. I clasp my hands against my throat and just gape at it.

Then they all start coming out, creeping out of their hollows, scurrying out of the shadows of the alleys, thumping up out of the coal holes of houses, surging from the darkness of drains and sewers.

The rat that touched me has stopped. It twitches. Suddenly I see to my horror that it is dripping blood from its mouth. Abruptly it spins round on its little pink feet and falls on to its side, motionless.

There is nowhere to go to get away from them. They are everywhere, and they are tottering and collapsing just like the first one. I find that I am moaning. I only realise it after a few moments.

'Emily! Whatever is the matter?' Roger takes hold of both my shoulders and gives me a little shake. 'Are you ill?'

I cannot believe that he is unable to see them. I gesture with both my hands all around us. A careering rat crashes into his foot and almost somersaults into the gutter. He glances down.

'There! Did you feel that?' I almost scream at him.

'Feel . . . ? How do you mean?'

'You looked down, Roger. You looked at your foot. Why did you look at your foot?' I gabble. He shakes his head.

'I can't remember. I think a muscle twitched in my ankle or something . . .'

The rats are piling up in the gutters. They are dying hideously at the entrances to alleys, contorted and bloody. A terrible smell drifts down the hill, the smell of tallow candles. I hold my hands over my mouth and nose and find that tears are pouring into them. Roger's fingers are digging into my shoulders now, and his tone is ferocious.

'Emily, *what can you see?*'

'Rats. I can see rats, Roger. They're dying all around us. I can't believe you can't see them. I think they're dying of plague, just like it said on the television . . .'

He looks down. He looks all around him, his expression bewildered and apprehensive. Then he lets go of my shoulders and takes hold of my hand.

'Emily, we're going to run. We're going to run all the way up the hill to the museum, as fast as we can. Come on!' He breaks into a trot, pulling me behind him, his feet barely missing the scurrying, staggering little bodies as they swarm at our feet. I stumble in my efforts to avoid them. At last we reach the top of the hill. As the darkness has deepened the artificial light of the lamps has created a feeling of complete unreality, and I wonder if I have now gone completely off my head.

Was the idea of rats planted in my mind by the news broadcast I saw just before we came out? Is this the extent to which fevered imagination can go?

Roger drags me round the back of the museum and through a small door next to a high, lighted window. I am trembling and sobbing as we slam the door behind us. Roger leans against it, wheezily out of breath.

'There,' he gasps. 'There.' We wait a moment and get our breath back.

There are several people already in the lighted room. A lot of comfortable chairs are arranged round low coffee tables.

'Hello Roger.'

'Hi Roger!'

There are crisps and biscuits on the tables. Under his breath Roger says, 'This is the main society's fortnightly meeting. However I also want you to come to the Beggarsgate Group afterwards. It meets in the back of the candle shop. Please don't mention this to anyone unless they mention it to you.' He raises his voice. 'This is Emily. She is interested in local history and would like to join our society.'

I sit down in a chair in the far corner and look round. There are several faces here that I recognise. Miss Patel nods to me and smiles. The proprietor of the candle shop to whom I spoke this morning raises her eyebrows and asks, 'Any sign of your cat?' I shake my head.

The Rodriguez boy who is in my class at school is there. He looks surprised to see me. 'Hi, Emily.'

Somewhere in the museum a clock chimes eight. Evelyn, the grey-haired woman whom I saw at reception this morning, starts the meeting with apologies from

Alice Smith for her absence, and a report on her health.

'. . . the odd thing which the doctors apparently can't understand,' she concludes, 'is that Alice seems to have bubonic plague, the sort spread by rodent fleas, whereas what Geeta's mother and everyone in that area had was pneumonic plague, the sort that goes straight into the lungs. Anyway, we'll leave that to the doctors to worry about. The main thing is that she's getting better.'

The meeting continues with various matters of local interest, an archaeological dig taking place on a demolition site behind the fire station, a Roman coin found in someone's garden, the publicity involving the park and the plague pit. Coffee is served half way through.

'I didn't know you were interested in history,' Matthew Rodriguez says to me. 'I got the impression that you slept through history lessons.'

I still feel very wobbly and all I really want to do is look out through the door and see if the rats are still there. 'Oh . . .' I answer him absentmindedly. 'Well, I'm just trying this out.'

'Great. Are you going anywhere afterwards?'

'Er . . . well I think Roger might have something lined up.'

'You're going somewhere with Roger afterwards?' Matthew Rodriguez looks at me closely. I frown and start to move away.

'Just something . . . I'm not quite sure what . . .'

He interrupts me, lowering his voice. 'Is it the Beggarsgate Group?'

I nod. He says nothing then, but gives me an intense stare and turns away. Evelyn calls us all to order and the meeting resumes.

When we emerge an hour later, the rats have all gone. I step shakily through the patches of light and dark, round to the front of the museum. A group of people from the society chats by the gate as the others disperse. Frances, the woman from the candle shop, is talking to a thin elderly man referred to as the major. Miss Patel is asking Matthew Rodriguez where his homework is. Roger is chatting in a group with Evelyn and two younger women.

I stand apart, staring up and down the street, looking for piles of rat corpses. I can hardly believe that they have all disappeared.

When everyone else has gone, the group by the gate makes its way over to the candle shop. Inside, Frances leads us all through to a small room at the back and lights beeswax candles in tall iron candelabra all round the room. We sit down, and I notice that people are looking at me curiously.

'I'd like to introduce Emily to the Beggarsgate Group,' says Roger. 'She has seen the beggars.'

Seventeen

I LOOK ROUND THE CIRCLE OF FACES, AMAZED. They look back at me, waiting. I feel hot and confused, unsure of what they expect me to say. The candles flicker. The flames seem too many, too bright.

I look at Roger. 'Have they . . . ?' I indicate the other people in the room.

'Yes,' replies Roger. 'They have all seen the beggars.' He looks round the group and says to them, 'Emily has also . . .' Here he pauses and glances uncertainly back at me. ' . . . seen the rats.'

Nobody says anything, but I can feel the surge of excitement.

'Tell us about it, Emily,' says Miss Patel at last, into the silence. The candles flare up in a sudden draught from the back of the shop. I shade my eyes. They feel sore. My headache has come back quite badly. I turn to Roger again.

'Does everyone here see the beggars like you do, Roger? Just faintly, like a bad film?' I have to know this, before I tell them what I see. I have to know how odd my revelations are going to sound.

'It varies, Emily.' Evelyn the reeptionist speaks before Roger can. 'Some of us hear them and smell them too.'

'Some of us have evidence of vermin in our houses, as well,' adds Roger, 'but we don't know if they are twentieth century vermin or part of the phenomenon.

What I thought were mouse droppings are, I think now, most probably rat droppings, after speaking to your rat catcher.'

'And have any of you ever actually touched . . .' My voice dries up as I remember Seth's grip on my arm as he dragged me away from Matchlock, and Pardoner's shaggy fur under my palms.

They are replying, some nodding, some shaking their heads, but I turn away, because the draught from the back of the shop is blowing on my neck now, making it ache, and making the candles billow. Some of the flames stream horizontally, then go out. Smoke scented with rosemary, lavender and beeswax curls upwards into a haze in the centre of the room. Then Seth walks in through the back door.

I jump to my feet. I am speechless, though a faint gasp comes out of my mouth. He is large, real and human. His face glistens with sweat. His foot scuffs up the edge of the carpet. He is solid, and not in any way a ghost. He is as he must have been when plague walked the streets. This is not me time-slipping back into the past, but time itself slipping forward. Seth is an ordinary human being from a place in history that never went away.

Vaguely I am aware of people talking to me. I face Seth and just stare at him. There is an expression of be-wilderment on his face.

'What has happened here?' he asks, looking around. I become aware of Matthew next to me. Seth nods to him. I look from one to the other.

'Can you see him?' I ask Matthew.

'Yes.'

'Come on, you two,' calls Evelyn. 'No going off in huddles on your own!'

I look back at the assembled group. They are smiling and waiting for Matthew and me to sit down. It is plain that they cannot see Seth. I turn back to Seth. He holds out his hand.

'Come with me?' he says.

I stand very still. I hear the tone of the voices behind me change to puzzlement and anxiety. Matthew takes hold of my arm.

'No,' I reply to Seth. 'No, I don't think I can.'

Today he is wearing silver buckled shoes instead of boots, and I see that his dark green breeches end just below the knee, revealing tan coloured stockings. He also has on a different coat, deep reddish brown and cut away from the front to show off his frilly white shirt. He is dressed up. He looks beautiful. It seems possible too that he might be wearing a wig, the same dark colour as his hair. I gaze at him, overwhelmed.

'Emily!' Suddenly Roger is shaking me. Why is Roger always shaking me? '*Emily*! What can you see?'

Seth takes hold of both my hands now, pulling me away from Roger and Matthew and drawing me towards the back of the shop.

'No, Seth!' It is Matthew Rodriguez's voice. Seth frowns at him in surprise, then ignores him.

He does not look like a murderer tonight. He does not look like a grief-crazed cat lover either. Around me, irritating voices, far off voices, like those of unpractised ghosts, are twittering and nagging.

'Emily, Emily,' they are saying.

I disregard the voices and walk with Seth to where a long curtain hides the back door of the shop. He sweeps the curtain aside. The door is standing open. From outside comes a fitful light and the disgusting smell of tallow candles.

Through the open door I can feel the night. It feels strange, a different night. A cool breeze blows in and soothes my headache. I hesitate, one foot on the step, one

—— 104 ——

on the cobblestones of the yard. Seth offers his arm to help me down the step, as if I were delicate, or hobbled by fragile shoes and long skirts.

I do not take his arm.

'Why do you want me to come with you?' I ask him.

He pauses, then shakes his head. 'I need to talk to you. I need to understand better . . .'

Then grossly, roughly, an arm comes between us.

'*No*, Seth!' It is Matthew Rodriguez. 'Get away from her. You don't understand what you're doing. She can't go with you.'

Matthew has surprising strength. He nearly pulls my arm out of its socket as he drags me backwards into the shop. I fight him, in a fury. Inside, shocked faces are watching us, and Miss Patel moves to intervene.

'You *can't* go with him,' Matthew hisses as I smack him across the ear and Miss Patel finally drags him off. 'Don't you understand? *That's* what happened to Alice Smith.'

Our journey back down the hill is slow. For one thing I now feel quite ill: sick, aching and miserable. I realise I must be starting flu. For another, there is so much to say, as I walk between Roger and Matthew Rodriguez.

I have apologised for hitting Matthew. He has apologised for wrenching my arm. An abbreviated version of the events of the past few weeks, right from the first moment of strangeness in Jonah's room, has been given to the Beggarsgate Group. There is frenzied speculation about Seth and his cat. I have explained that my mother, brother and a number of other people have all seen Pardoner, so he is clearly not a ghost, and that my mother also saw the black rat that appeared out of our chimney. There were gasps and moans of horror as I told them about the dying rats on the hill this evening.

The hill seems normal now, empty of all animal life except for number ninety-five's Siamese cat. I cannot understand how creatures of such writhing reality can have vanished. I find myself scanning the gutters for signs of hair or blood. There is nothing.

'Tell me about Alice,' I say to Matthew as his house and mine come into sight. He hesitates. Roger replies instead.

'She was obsessed,' he says shortly.

'We think she was the only other person to see Seth.' Matthew slows his pace as he speaks. 'There was certainly someone, anyway, and we assume it was probably Seth since he seems attractive to women and girls, in rather a cheap and obvious way.'

I see Roger stifle a smile.

Matthew continues. 'She wouldn't say much about him, except that he was someone who needed help.'

'Maybe it wasn't Seth,' puts in Roger. 'He sounds to me like a person who's quite capable of helping himself.' The memory of Seth in my kitchen, his head in his hands, flits across my mind.

Matthew shrugs. 'Well, as you say, she was obsessed. Miss Patel took her to India to try and take her mind off the infatuation.' He gestures with his hand. 'Roger tried to talk sense into her too, but Alice had almost reached the point where she didn't want to live in this century any more. She wanted to go back to be with this person, whoever he was.'

'She almost got her wish not to live in this century,' puts in Roger brusquely. 'She almost ended up not living in any century at all.'

Matthew turns to face me. We are outside my house now. 'No one knows whether she picked up plague in India or . . .'

Roger cuts across him. 'It must have been India, Matthew.' He glances at me and gives Matthew a warning look. 'You can't pick up plague from ghosts. I know it's bubonic rather than pneumonic that she's caught, but everyone knows they do run side by side. You only have to read accounts of the Great Plague of London to come across what are obviously descriptions of bubonic, pneumonic and septicaemic plague, all running side by side as complications of each other.'

Matthew's mother comes out on to their step on the opposite side of the road and calls, 'Telephone, Matthew!'

He says a quick goodbye and rushes off. Roger turns to go into his house, waiting while I find my key and open our front door. Then he gives a little wave and a conciliatory smile and watches from the monochrome shadows of the street light while I go in.

Eighteen

*I*T IS DARK IN THE HOUSE. MUM AND JONAH MUST have gone to bed. I close the door behind me and stand for a moment in the darkness, appreciating the relief it gives my aching head and sore eyes.

I think of Seth, and wonder if he can possibly understand what is happening. To me, he exists in the past, which, bizarre though the concept might be, is at least recognisable because it has already happened and is recorded in history books. To him, though, I exist in the future, which must be completely strange and unknowable. Am I perhaps to him just some sort of dream creature? He has talked of seeing me in dreams.

I move across the room slowly, in the darkness, blinking repeatedly as my eyes start to feel more comfortable.

It seems to me that I am seeing Seth at different times in the past, and not necessarily in the right order. Could this account for his astonishingly changed state on the night when I surprised him in our house? Was he then in the grip of some future grief that has not yet happened to the Seth of tonight? Is it possible, in fact, that our encounters are occurring in *reverse order*? Could I be *working my way backwards* into the past? That is what happens when you do go backwards, isn't it. You encounter the most recent first.

I stand very still in the black silence and grapple

with this idea. That would mean that in the right order, tonight's Seth would be followed by brisk Seth of the night of the dead cart, followed by grief-crazed burglar Seth suffering the aftermath of some terrible event, and later, serious Seth looking for his cat in the alley.

'Come with me?' he said tonight, and he made it sound easy. Could I have gone? Was it physically possible? I know what lay in that yard behind the candle shop tonight. It was London in the year of the Great Plague. I could smell it and feel it. Would a step forwards on to the cobblestones have been for me a step backwards across the centuries? The thought is terrifying, yet . . . I wanted to go. I have only had glimpses of the past so far. This, I think, would have been different.

Roger and Matthew said that Alice Smith was obsessed. I can understand how someone could be, and I know that I must now meet her as soon as possible. Roger referred to 'rare people' who just stumble right into the past here on Hound Hill. He must have meant Alice. Am I one of those people too?

I am standing in the middle of the room and I reach out to the small table that stands behind the sofa, to switch on the table lamp with the stained glass shade — the wall lights will be too bright for my sore eyes — and I find . . . nothing. Puzzled, I grope around. We are not near enough to the street lamp for any light from it to enter, and anyway the curtains are drawn. I circle one arm through the darkness. No, the lamp is not there. Mum must have been rearranging things. I will have to switch the main lights on after all. I move back to the door and flick the switch.

I am in the wrong house.

This thought lasts only a moment. I think, oh, how embarrassing. Then I think, but how can it be, when my key fitted the lock and anyway Roger saw me go into the house?

Once, long ago, when Jonah and I were small, we were prescribed some medicine, a decongestant or something, and it gave us nightmares and hallucinations. Jonah saw giant spiders running up the walls and I saw the furniture marching round the room. It is like that now, an experience of seeing what cannot be so.

It seems as if everything has changed in the room. The television, video and music centre have all gone. So have the two stained glass table lamps and the two valuable figurines that Mum inherited from her great aunt. The bareness of the room suggests that other things have gone too, though I can't for the moment think what.

Instead, there is strange furniture here. Under the window is a carved wooden chest on legs which I recognise as the Restoration coffer from the antique shop. In a corner under the standard lamp by the kitchen doorway is an ornately carved chair with dull red velvet upholstery and fringes, which looks for some reason familiar. A heavy oak stool stands by the fireplace. I remain motionless and just stare, almost feeling as if I want to give the room a chance to return to normal.

There has to be a reason for this. Our modern equipment has gone. Old things have taken its place.

'Seth?' I whisper cautiously. The house is silent apart from the ticking of the grandfather clock. I move across the room, touching the delicately carved leaves on the panels of the coffer, lifting its lid to reveal an empty interior, stroking the dented velvet seat of the chair, riffling the fringe in the middle of its back. 'Seth?'

Pardoner's saucer of milk is still in a corner of the kitchen, gone a little crusty round the edges now. I tip the remains down the sink. In the kitchen the microwave is nowhere to be seen.

Tiptoeing, hardly able to breathe, I cross the living room again and make my way upstairs. For a moment I think I will not be brave enough to turn the corner of the stairs, in case there is someone there — Matchlock perhaps? — standing at the top looking down at me. The treads creak underfoot.

Then I hear Mum's bedsprings squeaking as she turns over in her narrow bed in the cupboard bedroom. It is followed by one of the deep whiffling sighs she gives when she is sleeping. I move forward and hear faint music coming from Jonah's room. He must be awake. The relief I feel is indescribable. I never thought I would be glad to hear Motorhead played even as quietly as this. I stop outside his door and without giving myself time to think — no, I do think: I think what if the changes downstairs are in some way matched by something unimaginable in Jonah's room — I knock sharply on the door.

There is no reply. I raise my hand to knock again, but I am almost too afraid to do it. The only light reaching up here is an indirect luminescence from round the corner of the stairs. I could switch my bedroom light on. I stretch out my hand but withdraw it quickly. I can't reach, and it's just too dark to move to that end of the landing. Abruptly I hammer on Jonah's door then stand back, looking to and fro, my arms wrapped round me.

'Huh?' It is faint, but it is Jonah's voice. I open the door and walk, very slowly, into the dimly lighted room.

I have never seen Jonah like this. He is lying on his bed, on his back, his face swollen and red. Silent tears are running from his eyes down the sides of his face, into his ears and soaking down through his hair on to the pillow. I don't think I have seen Jonah cry since he was about eight. It is somehow a more painful thing to see a boy cry

— 111 —

when he has tiny pinpricks of stubble on his chin and a scatter of spots across the side of his neck. It clenches my stomach and makes my chest ache.

'Jonah?' I whisper. He struggles to see me, pushing himself up against his pillows.

'Emily.'

I cross to the bed and sit on the edge of it and take hold of his hand. He looks far more vulnerable now than he ever did when he was small. I suppose I should have seen this coming. Today's visit to Dad was the culmination of a lot of very bad days.

I realise I must wait before asking him about what has happened downstairs. I mop his face with one of his discarded socks. Then I see what I had not noticed before. There is a bottle of beer on Jonah's bedside table. As if he knows I am going to stop him, he reaches out for it and quickly levers off the top with a pair of compasses from his maths set.

'Jonah, don't . . .' The bedside light shines through the bottle. The beer is golden brown, a colour like the peaty streams we paddled in during our childhood holidays in the north, the colour of safe, happy days when parents stayed together and time stayed where it was supposed to be.

The bottle has a mock mediaeval label with a picture of an unconvincing monk and a stained glass window. It is called Trappist Ale. Jonah lifts the bottle to his mouth but I grab his wrist and the Trappist Ale sprays across his face, going everywhere except into his mouth. He stares at me speechlessly and the strong smelling beer drips off his eyelashes, joining the tears.

'That would only make you feel worse, Jonah.'

He turns his face away from me and cradles the bottle against his chest.

'Jonah, has something terrible happened? Everything

is different downstairs. Have we . . . gone back into the past?'

'What? What do you mean? What past?'

Surreptitiously he raises the bottle to his lips again, like a determined baby. This time I take it away from him completely. I sniff it. It smells disgusting. I move to put the bottle on top of his chest of drawers, the only surface in the room with any space, but abruptly I change my mind and go and stuff it into a corner by the door.

'The furniture is different downstairs, Jonah.' I come back and sit on one of his packing cases. 'The television and other things have gone.'

'Oh.' He sighs. 'We've been burgled, Em. Mum and I had to go next door to Mrs Bagling's because she had a dead rat in her drain, and while we were out, someone broke the kitchen window and got in and ransacked the place. It was probably that boy you saw the other night.'

I stare at Jonah in dismay.

'They took my CD player and your clock radio,' he adds.

'But what about the other things, Jonah? The old furniture that wasn't here before?'

'Oh, that's the stuff Mum bought this morning. It was delivered by the woman from the antique shop just after you and Roger left this evening.' Jonah gets up and searches in his dressing gown pocket for his cigarettes and then remembers that he gave them away. A look of complete desolation crosses his face.

I have an unexpected memory of him as a toddler. 'Look after Jonah,' Mum would say if she wanted to get on with some job round the house, and I would be overcome with the awesome responsibility of guarding this person who was even smaller than I was.

I am shocked at myself. What am I doing? Jonah

— 113 —

sleeps in this room where unknown terrors lurk behind his chest of drawers and I have neglected to tell him or protect him. Whatever it is, dreams, imagination or the Beggarsgate phenomenon, the sense of harm in Jonah's room is unmistakable.

One of my main reactions to meeting the other members of the Beggarsgate Group tonight was relief. At least I am not alone, I thought. I am not mad. Somehow Roger did not count as a reliable witness, and I had had it constantly at the back of my mind that people who hear voices and see visions tend to be quickly prescribed medication and care in the community. It is a relief to know that what I am experiencing is a real phenomenon. Yet so many things still remain unexplained, and the horror in Jonah's room is one of them.

'Jonah.' I sit back on the edge of his bed in a position where I can keep an eye on his chest of drawers. It seems belatedly very important that Jonah should know what so many other people already know, because tonight the situation feels more dangerous than ever. It appears to me that somehow the scene is being set for something — what, I do not know. We have been stripped of the protection of modern things, electronics and twentieth century gadgets, and we have brought in the old, the carved, the antiquities that Seth and Matchlock would have known. The Restoration coffer is empty, but it contains history, and it is frightening.

I take off my coat and straighten Jonah's bedclothes and fold up a crumpled Metallica t-shirt. I think of Roger, folding, tidying. 'Jonah,' I say carefully, 'there are some things I had better tell you.'

Nineteen

*T*HAT NIGHT I DREAM THAT THE PLAGUE PIT IS waking. Something is stirring underground. The soil starts moving. I wake with a scream and find that my heart is thumping wildly.

It is the depths of the night. There are no comforting red digits from my clock radio, and I remember that it has been stolen. What time is it? It feels like two or three o'clock in the morning. I lie very still, waiting to become calmer, for my pulse to slow and my breathing to settle down again. There is the faintest creak over by the door. I tense, and move my head slowly so that both my ears are freed from the muffling of the pillow. The courtyard lamp outside throws a faint light against my curtains, but not enough to penetrate the room. Yet I am sure that I can see something there, over by the door.

I stare, widening my eyes and trying to force them to see what they cannot. The creak comes again, and there is something else now. It is the sound of breathing. Someone is definitely there. Soft breathing is coming from the dark shape that is not my dressing gown, over by the door.

I daren't move, or switch my light on, or speak.

'Are you awake?' it asks. I give a strangled shout and reach out roughly to switch my bedside light on.

'Jonah! How could you do that? I was scared stiff!'

In the light from my lamp I see my brother standing

just inside my doorway. He looks pale and tired but he is smiling.

'Sorry. I didn't mean to frighten you. I wasn't sure whether to disturb you or not, but I thought you'd want to know, Em. The cat has come back.'

Amazed and elated, I follow Jonah downstairs, but as I do so, I cannot stop myself from thinking, is this it then? Is this the start of whatever the scene has been set for? If it is, who — or what — might arrive next?

I have 'Greensleeves' on my brain. It was on my brain all evening and it still won't go away.

Pardoner is on the hearthrug drinking some milk that Jonah has poured into one of Mum's best bone china saucers. We kneel on either side of the cat, stroking its rough coat and uneven crewcut head. Pardoner is purring into the milk with a sound like the tiny bubbles in simmering soup. I go and turn the catch on the cat flap so that he cannot get out again, and then come back and sit on the newly arrived antique stool by the fireplace.

Jonah looks up at me. 'What you were telling me earlier, Em . . .'

'Yes.'

'I'm not imagining it? About beggars and rats and Seth . . .'

'I should have told you sooner.'

'And . . . my room?'

'Yes.'

'So Pardoner . . .' He picks up the cat and sits on the sofa with it on his lap. 'Pardoner is . . . a ghost?'

We both look at the cat and then at each other and back at the cat. Pardoner is settling down to sleep, turning round, kneading at Jonah's green dressing gown with his disproportionately large, fluffy paws, purring, stopping to scratch his ear. Pardoner is not a ghost.

—— 116 ——

I shrug. 'I don't pretend to understand any of it, Jonah. I just thought you ought to know, because I think whatever is in your room is different. I think it's something really frightening.' I remember my sleep-walking dream of Seth and the stone dripping with blood, and I wonder if it was any more than just a dream. So much here is not what it seems.

Jonah shifts on the sofa, leans back among the cushions, strokes the cat. Pardoner has gone to sleep.

'I can scarcely believe it, Em. Yet . . . I can believe it. Now that you have said all that, I suppose I sort of half knew there was something. Who says what ghosts are supposed to look like, after all?'

'Roger thinks it isn't ghosts. He thinks it's the past which simply hasn't gone away properly. Maybe because the time of the Great Plague was so dreadful that it can't be forgotten.'

We don't go back to bed that night. Instead we sit up drinking coffee and talking. As dawn pales the curtains we switch off the electric lights and watch the shadows inch back from the corners of the room, from the spaces where our electronic gadgets were, and from the new contours created by the ancient chair, the stool and the Restoration coffer.

Mum gets up early and is obviously very upset. She rings the insurance company's emergency number and decides that we will wait until the week after next before replacing the stolen items, in case they're found in the meantime.

The police were here last night while I was out, but they call again this morning to talk to me. Mum wants me to tell the two young policemen about the boy I saw with the video in his arms. It seems ridiculous, but there is nothing else I can do. I describe Seth, knowing that they will be unlikely to catch him, since having lived more than three hundred years ago is probably the best alibi you can have.

Mum's eyes are red rimmed and swollen. 'To think we were only next door,' she keeps saying. 'And the house-warming party is tomorrow.'

So it is. I had forgotten. Monday is Mum's day off work this week and school is to be closed for staff training on Tuesday, so it had seemed a good day, until this happened.

'We'll borrow Roger's stereo,' says Mum when the police have gone. She turns to me. 'Em, would you go round and see Mrs Bagling, please? She was very upset yesterday about that dead rat. Tell her I've spoken to our rat catcher and he'll be round tomorrow, and ask her if she needs anything.'

As I go out I see Matthew Rodriguez across the road. He comes over to me and smiles.

'You OK, Emily?'

'Yes thanks.' I tell him about our robbery and he says that two other houses up the hill were burgled last week.

'Are you coming to our house-warming party?'

'Mum and Dad are. Do you want me to come too? I will if you like.'

'Why weren't you coming?' I feel slightly offended. I don't want him to do me any favours.

He shrugs, rams his hands in his pockets and kicks at a tuft of grass between the paving stones. 'The truth? Oh well, here goes another promising relationship . . . you seemed like such a stuck-up public school kid . . .'

I laugh, wave and turn away to knock on Mrs Bagling's door. 'Please yourself,' I call over my shoulder.

An upstairs window opens. 'Oh Emily, come in, dear. I'm up here.'

Mrs Bagling is in her cream and gilt bedroom. It is festooned with little lacy cushions and bowls of dried flowers. She is sitting at her dressing table sorting through her jewel box.

'Emily, I'm so upset by this business of the rat. My home help has always kept this place spotless. I never even see a spider or a fly, never mind rats . . . not that my eyesight is too good so I probably wouldn't anyway. Do you think these pearl earrings will go?'

I consider her outfit of sequinned mauve lace and nod. 'Yes. They'll be nicely understated.' I pass on Mum's messages. 'Can I get you anything, Mrs Bagling?'

The old woman seems uncharacteristically agitated today. She presses a hand to her forehead. Powder is flaking from her nose. I wonder suddenly if she has more reasons to be upset about the rat than just the obvious ones. Could Mrs Bagling possibly also be aware of the Beggarsgate phenomenon? She has shown no sign before.

'Dear, would you get me some headache tablets from my bathroom cabinet, please?' she asks. 'I think I might be starting the flu.'

'It must be going round.' I go to fetch the tablets and a glass of water. 'I haven't been feeling too good myself for a few days.' As I say this I find that I am shivering, despite feeling rather hot. I return to the bedroom and ask cautiously, 'Mrs Bagling, that rat, did you keep it to show to the rat catcher?'

Her hand flutters to her throat. 'I think your mother or Jonah did. I think they wrapped it up and put it by the dustbin.'

Even more cautiously I ask, 'Mrs Bagling, I was just wondering . . . have you ever seen anything else . . . ?'

She spins round in her chair. 'Don't!'

I jump in surprise and the water splashes on to my hand. Something shocking is happening to Mrs Bagling's face, and I realise to my horror that she is terribly angry. I put the tablets and the glass carefully down in front of her.

'Mrs Bagling, I'm sorry . . . I only wanted to know . . .'

'*No*, Emily! *No*, I have seen nothing! Nothing! I have never seen anything, do you understand me? It's a lot of nonsense. Speak of the devil and he will appear. Don't say a word more!'

I realise in dismay that she is on the verge of tears. Her eyes are shimmering and her hands are trembling. She picks up the pearl earrings with her glass of water and I am only just in time to stop her from swallowing them instead of the tablets.

'Mrs Bagling!'

Dusty tears well down her cheeks. I put my arm round her.

'I'm sorry. I'm sorry,' I whisper. 'You don't have to talk about it. Of course you don't.'

There is a silence, during which Mrs Bagling blows her nose on a lace handkerchief and takes her tablets. Eventually, to break the silence, I tell her about our robbery. I can see that she is shocked. I want to ask her more about the rat, to find out what sort of rat it was and what it seems to have died of, but judging by her recent reaction, I think I probably know already.

'There are some very wicked people about,' says Mrs Bagling at last. 'I hope the police catch the thieves and get your things back for you. Is there anything I can do? I told your mother I'd bake some of my special homemade bread for the party, so I'll be round later to talk about how many loaves she'll need.'

In the end Mrs Bagling comes back with me. I leave her and Mum in the living room making shopping lists for tomorrow's party, and go upstairs to find Jonah. Together we creep out of the back door to Mrs Bagling's dustbin.

'I want to know if it was one of the rats from last night, Jonah,' I whisper, glancing back to make sure our departure has not been observed. 'I want to know if it died of plague.'

'There.' Jonah points to the newspaper package tucked behind the dustbin. I remember the rats of Beggarsgate, spiralling on their tiny paws, falling dead at my feet with blood streaming from their noses and mouths. I reach down before I can lose courage.

'Let me,' says Jonah. We stand in the unsavoury alley and between us we unwrap the tightly rolled package of last Sunday's *News of the World*. We pull apart the pages one by one. The rat has been wrapped neatly, in layers, a bizarre mockery of the newspaper-wrapped fish and chips which we eat sitting high on clean, wind-scoured rocks at Great Grandmother Strachan's.

'Vicar's shame', says a headline. 'MP's secret life'. 'Princess joins Communist Party'. 'Flogging is good for you, says headmaster'.

The pages peel away, falling with their scandals and ruined lives on to the cobblestones at our feet, and there is nothing inside.

Twenty

*I*T'S THE HELPLESSNESS THAT'S WORST. IT'S always the helplessness that feels so frightening, isn't it, when you really don't understand something. I want to be brave. I want to be much braver than I am. I'm sure I used to be braver than this. Where has it all gone, that upbeat attitude? Today the world seems absolutely bleak.

I am getting ready for school. I go downstairs. Mum has been making a fuss because I won't eat any breakfast. Even the idea of food revolts me this morning. I just want to drink glass after glass of water, and even then I still feel thirsty.

There is some sort of unidentifiable sweet smell in the house. I stand at the bend of the stairs and sniff. It is almost familiar, but I can't quite place it. Then I remember. It is hawthorn, may blossom, the smell of the hedges round Great Grandmother Strachan's house.

This seems inexplicable. There are certainly no may hedges round here, and even if there were, it is totally the wrong season for blossom. I go into the kitchen and mention this strange phenomenon to Mum, but she can't smell it at all. Nor can Jonah, even though it is so strong and seems to be getting stronger.

I can't seem to get myself organised for school this morning. If only I could throw off this dreadful gloom that has settled on me, or make sense of my feeling of apprehension. I look round at our small, ordinary house, at our quite nice furniture, our slightly shabby rugs and cushions, breakfast dishes, notes stuck to the fridge, newspapers and post in a heap by the door. There is nothing I can point to and say help! Look at that! Save me from that!

'Come on, Em,' says Jonah, standing by the door.

'I'm coming,' I snap at him, annoyed, but still somehow not quite able to gather up all my things and get out of the house. Jonah picks up the post and puts it on the telephone table, then leans against the doorpost reading the paper. I catch a glimpse of a headline: 'Two more plague cases in London'. I cram my lunchbox into my bag and call goodbye to Mum. She comes over to the door to see us out. She still has this habit of waving to us and we just can't seem to get her out of it.

'Emily, are you all right?' She stares at me closely. 'You look sort of . . . grey.' She puts a hand out and touches my cheek.

'Thanks, Mum!' I reply, trying to make a joke of it, but the truth of the matter is that I feel sort of grey.

A strong wind is blowing again this morning. The street is full of movement and dirt. It looks really depressing. Bits of newspaper are clinging to the air, flat and skimming along, old news and old sorrows pushed in your face by the bullying wind. The Rodriguezes' chimney is smoking and the air currents have created horizontal slices of smoke, so you can see the shape of the wind. You can see the invisible here on Hound Hill.

Mrs Bagling comes out of her house and jogs down to ours. She is wearing a gold lamé tracksuit. She takes one look at me and says, 'That child's not well.' Mum puts her hand to my forehead, frowning.

'I think you're right. You might be better off not going in to school today, Em. You do feel a bit feverish. What a shame, on the day of the party too.'

'After I've waited all this time,' groans Jonah, turning on his heel. He blows us stagey kisses and rolls his eyes as he turns the corner into the alley.

'I wonder if we should postpone the party,' considers Mum as we go back into the house and I sink down on the sofa.

'No!' I look at her pleadingly, then try to moderate my tone. 'No really, please don't. That would be such a shame.'

After all, whatever is waiting to happen surely won't dare to, with a house full of people.

I go to bed for a while and lie listening to the wind, but gradually I become aware of a closer sound. It is as if the wind were in the walls, a sighing along the pipes and in the radiators.

'The central heating's playing up again,' grumbles Mum when I go downstairs and ask her if she can hear it. 'I put it on because of your flu.'

In the kitchen the fire is roaring up the chimney. Roger is making coffee.

'Do *you* think it's the central heating, Roger?' I ask him pointedly. He concentrates on the coffee, meticulously pressing down the plunger in the coffee pot.

'Possibly not,' he replies, then looks up at me. He raises his eyebrows. 'Do you think it's the central heating, Emily?'

A fit of ice cold shivering suddenly shakes me, like a dog playing with a stick. I stare back at him.

'No.'

'Of course it's the central heating,' says Mum, sounding puzzled. 'What else could it be? Listen to it. It's right there in the pipes. That boiler's so old it might have to be replaced before the very cold weather comes. It is funny though. It almost sounds like voices.'

Mrs Bagling, who has been baking bread in our kitchen range ever since she arrived earlier, laughs brightly. 'My, what an active imagination you have, Alexandra. I can't hear a thing.' She looks straight at the wall where the sound is loudest. 'No, not a thing. Well, maybe just a little bit of air in the pipes.' She smiles down at Pardoner who is playfully attacking the pompoms on her turquoise satin slippers. 'Your cat is a lot better, isn't he.' She opens one of the black iron doors, releasing billows of heat, and draws out a tray of steaming golden loaves. 'My goodness, Alexandra, I wish I had bread ovens like these. They're wonderful.'

Mum and Roger move over to the bread as if magnetised. 'That smells absolutely amazing,' says Mum. 'It will be perfect with just cheese and wine for the party.'

Mrs Bagling whips a tea towel off another tray of yeasty mounds that have been rising on the kitchen table and puts it into the bread oven, leaning back from the heat. Her face is red and shiny, her powder long gone. She swings the black iron door shut with a clang.

The smell of newly baked bread fills the house. I cannot understand why it smells so disgusting to me when everyone else is going into raptures over it. Mum opens the back door and the smell floods out into the alley. Roger pours coffee and we move towards the living room to drink it.

'Sarah . . .' The voice is no more than a whisper. 'Oh, Sarah . . .'

I stand completely still in the kitchen doorway.

'You know what you could do,' Mrs Bagling is saying as she settles herself on the sofa. 'Hernando Rodriguez is a plumber. You could ask him to take a look at your plumbing if you think you've got air in the pipes.'

'I think it's getting worse.' Mum is frowning. 'It's never sounded like this before.'

The smell of baking bread swirls about my head and I sit down on one of the kitchen chairs.

'Seth?' I whisper. I jump with fright as Roger comes back into the kitchen. The noise retreats to a breathy hum behind the plaster of the walls.

'Well?' I clasp my hands on the table and look up at him. He shakes his head and moves the baking tray of hot loaves so that it is exactly parallel to the edge of the table.

'I don't know,' he whispers.

Plague is on the television news at lunchtime. Two more Londoners, one in Stepney and one in Bethnal Green, have been confirmed as sufferers. They have been nowhere near India.

Roger arrives back with shopping bags full of cheese and bottles of wine. He stands in the doorway, listening. 'How ironic,' he says. 'Those areas, and ours, were some of the worst hit during the Great Plague of London. They were called the liberties, or out-parishes, because they were outside the old city walls.'

'. . . and it has been confirmed that within the past fortnight both new sufferers visited the museum where the original contact worked,' the newscaster is continuing. 'Alice Smith is now recovering and the authorities are anxious to avoid any panic. However Hound Hill Museum has been closed until further notice and all staff are being given health checks.If anyone who has had contact with the original sufferer since her return from India is experiencing flu-like symptoms, they are advised to consult their doctor without delay . . .'

'Well, at least none of us has been in contact with her.'

Mum starts unloading the shopping bags. 'Have we?' Mrs Bagling and Roger shake their heads.

'I met Geeta Patel while I was out,' says Roger. 'She's been completely cleared. She'll be coming to the party.'

'Oh good.' Mum puts her hands on her hips and stares around at the array of food and drink. 'Thank you both so much for all your help. It's going to be a great night.'

Twenty-one

I GO BACK TO BED, TAKING A PINT GLASS OF WATER with me to try and quench my uncontrollable thirst. As I trudge up the stairs, clumsily slopping water on to my feet, the sounds seem to follow me, running up the stairs beside me. At the bend of the stairs I stand still to hear whether they stop too, but they just carry on as before, sighing and whispering.

I stop outside Jonah's room. I feel desperate. I want to confront the thing in there, but I dare not.

I sleep on and off through the afternoon. I am aware of being asleep, of feeling ill, of dreaming, of drifting in and out of dreams. Sometimes the sounds in the walls seem closer and louder and they wake me.

I sink into deeper sleep as evening approaches and the shadows extend across the floor. In my sleep I hear something scrabbling at my door. I hear the wind rising and howling round the house, like the wolves in fairy tales. I hear creakings in the chimney.

When I finally wake up, the room is full of the radiance of late evening. Outside in the courtyard the branches of the oak tree are being lashed about by the wind, and they create a fluttering pattern of light across my window. The noises in the pipes are almost drowned out now by the gusts of wind along the alleys.

Immediately I am hit by the shock of the smell. It is overwhelming, sweet, sickly, a florist's shop left to rot in a heatwave.

'Oh!' I gasp for breath. My chest hurts. As the wind drops briefly I hear the pipes tapping and stuttering more loudly than ever. I stagger out of bed and drag myself to the stairs. The wind gives a primitive roar and the whole house seems to rock.

'Mum!'

Sounds of music and laughter and voices are coming from downstairs. The party must have started. Mrs Bagling's head appears round the bend of the stairs.

'Oh Emily, you're up. Your mother didn't want to disturb you. How are you feeling?'

I hold on to the wall. Mrs Bagling frowns and comes up to me. 'I think I'd better get your mother, Emily. You really don't look well. You go back to bed, dear.'

A long, low groan comes from the wall next to me. I lurch away from it in fright. Mrs Bagling jumps then compresses her lips into a grim expression and stands rigidly in the middle of the stairs.

'The noises, Mrs Bagling . . .'

She clicks her tongue. 'I'm afraid Mr Rodriguez wasn't able to find anything wrong with the central heating. It's just as I said, nothing to worry about. Now you go back to bed, Emily. It might be that your mother will want to call the doctor . . .'

'No!' I shake my head and hold out my hand to stop her. The prospect of going back to bed and being alone there appals me. 'No, I'll get ready and come down to the party. Honestly, I'm all right, thank you, Mrs Bagling. Really.'

I go back into my room and feverishly drag on my favourite purple and lilac dress made of filmy Indian cotton. It has uneven layers of hemline and bits of ribbon in odd places. Normally this dress makes me feel good but this evening it feels garish and messy. I brush my

— 129 —

hair and wind it up into a bun on the back of my neck in an attempt to feel cooler, although I find that despite feeling hot I am now shivering uncontrollably.

'Emily! Get a move on!' shouts a voice. It sounds like Matthew Rodriguez. I go out of my bedroom and start to make my way downstairs. Once more I hold on to the wall because I am feeling very dizzy. The living room is candlelit and full of people talking and laughing and drinking. Over on the Restoration coffer Jonah is sitting with Pardoner, refilling people's wine glasses and reading a copy of *New Scientist*. I join him.

'Hi, Em. Did you know that alcohol is . . .' he quotes from the magazine, 'a liquid nerve toxin made from a microbial waste product?'

'Really?' exclaims Mum in an interested voice as she appears at his shoulder and reaches over to pour herself a generous glass of chardonnay. 'How are you, Em? What on earth is that extraordinary scent you're wearing?'

'Scent, Mum? I'm not wearing . . .' I realise as I say it that at last Mum must be able to smell the smell.

However, I never get the chance to say this, because at that moment I look over towards the front window, and in the last florid rays of the sunset I see a crowd of faces looking in.

My first thought is that these are more guests arriving, but as the nearest face pushes right up against the glass, I see that it is Matchlock.

My sharp intake of breath makes several people look round. I clench and unclench my hands, then take a step forward. Matchlock squashes his nose up against the glass and smiles a crooked smile, then bares his teeth at me. I take another step forward. Plague or no plague, that does it. It is time for confrontation. I cannot go on like this. I am going to get hold of Matchlock and drag him in here.

—— 130 ——

'Em?' I hear Jonah's voice behind me, then his hand is on my arm. 'Are you all right?' I turn to him.

'Can you see them?' I point. I notice with a sort of detached interest that my outstretched arm is shaking quite violently.

'See what?'

Jonah sounds completely bewildered, but as I summon all the strength in my trembling muscles I hear Roger's voice behind me.

'I can see them, Emily. Don't go out there.'

He is too late. I am out there and the door is caught by the wind and smashed back against the telephone table. The beggars of Beggarsgate turn towards me, their rags flapping wildly, their hair streaming across their faces. They are laughing.

The wind is bellowing in my ears and the orange moon is rising curved and crazy in a darkening sky. Rags of cloud go whirring across it. I have to lean forward just to stay upright. The garbled chatter of the party behind me mixes with the howling wind and the crowing walls. Above it all, the chimney makes the same slow creaking sound that I heard when I was in my bedroom.

This is such a strange and unusual sound that it catches my attention more than anything else, more than the beggars, the party guests, the rubbish flying by and Mum and Jonah who are trying to make me go back inside. I crane my neck and look up through the leaves and debris that are blowing past.

'Look!' I point again, shocked at what I see. The chimney is at a strange angle. 'Mum, look at the chimney!' But there is no time. As I speak, the chimney shifts. Some bricks fall loose. Gasps go up from the guests, more of whom have followed us out of the house to see what is going on. They start seizing hold of each other and backing away in disarray.

— 131 —

Strangely, there is still a thin haze of smoke coming out of the top of the chimney, but suddenly it is coming out of the sides instead, as the tall column of bricks starts to crumble.

I have no strength to move. Hands grab at me but it is too late to get away. The chimney is toppling now. A wild gust that nearly knocks me off my feet tilts the red-brown chimneypot. As I watch, it tumbles lopsidedly and crashes through the roof into Jonah's room.

The noise is thunderous. My eardrums resonate and the sound goes on as the rest of the chimney comes down in a storm of broken bricks and slates. Somewhere a window smashes. A piece of slate bounces off Mum's car and hits me on the shoulder. A brick narrowly misses my head, instead grazing my cheek and nose. The pain is intense, and now I join the clumsy, hasty movement away from the danger. Great clouds of dust fill the street, choking me and obscuring the moon. The wind sucks dust across the sky and forces grit and debris into my nose and eyes.

All round me people are coughing and crying out. I hear my name and Jonah's being called by Mum and Roger, but their voices are muffled and carried away by the wind.

When the bricks stop falling I turn and look back. Miraculously, nothing else has hit me. I look at the place where our chimney stood. The dust is like smoke, swirling and eddying now, adding to the growing darkness, but there is something else. It is something which was not there before. It is another chimney, visible faintly, where the first chimney stood before.

For a moment I think it is just the rough and broken stub of the previous chimney, but then I see that this is different. It is a short, twisted chimney, uneven and thick in construction, crooked like no other I have ever seen, as crooked as Matchlock's smile. Thick smoke is coming out of it, not decorous Coalite haze.

My headache clears, my thirst and dizziness go and I feel very much better.

Twenty-two

*T*HE DUST IS SETTLING. THE WIND IS DROPPING.
the scene around me emerges like shadows from
smoke. Gradually it becomes clearer. I am standing in a
tiny, narrow street that winds untidily up the hill, the
same hill, Hound Hill. I have not moved from where I
stood.

Nothing else is the same though, only the contour of
the land. Where our solid terraced houses stood, now
there are leaning, timber-framed houses jumbled
together and almost touching in places over the central
cobbles. These houses have small leaded windows of
thick greenish glass set high in dust-crusted walls. I
reach out and touch one of the walls. It feels coarse,
rough-plastered, splintery, real.

I experience a sense of absolute disbelief. This, definitely, has to be a dream or more probably, a nightmare.

I rub the grit from my eyes. A haze of smoke in the air
has replaced the dust from the chimney, and it is making
my eyes water. The last of the grit, the remains of my
own world, washes down my cheeks and is gone.

There is no one about. I look all round. My cheek
throbs where the brick caught it. I can hear the blood in
my veins gusting like the wind in the alleys. Far off down
the hill I can see the church spire. Behind it, in the west,
bloody shreds of sunset remain. In the east, to my back,
dark bruise-blue fills the sky.

Everything feels different. The sounds are different. There is no background hum. The smell is different, earthy and a bit decayed. Even the air on my skin feels different, soft and raw and warm like the air of a foreign country.

Everything is very still now that the wind has dropped. I stand under the overhanging gable of the nearest house. These houses seem very haphazardly built, with tiny alleys between them scarcely wide enough for a person to fit through. I look out across the cobbled street to the houses on the opposite side, which seem to be at least four storeys high, and see strange marks on their doors. I recognise the marks: huge red crosses and the badly written words 'Lord have mercy upon us'.

My breath catches in my throat. Lord have mercy upon us. So it has happened. This is not the past leaking forward into twentieth century Hound Hill. This *is* the past. This is London of the Plague Year, and I have stumbled back into it. I wrap my arms around myself and shiver. Lord have mercy upon us.

I stare up and down the hill. There is no one about. Do I want there to be anyone about? My mind is in turmoil. How can I ever get back? I am on the spot where my house stands, but my house is separated from me by more than three centuries. A terrible wave of longing for home swamps me. This place looks so different, yet behind the ramshackle chaos of buildings that I can see now, the outline of the street that I know is there, the ghost of future Hound Hill lurks in the curve of the road, the distant church spire and the shape of the hill.

This truly is a terrible place. The cobbles in the road are thick with filth: dung, discarded vegetable skins, chicken bones and other animal remains, broken pots and rotted pieces of wood. Down the middle, in an open drain, runs a trickle of evil smelling slime. Over it a thick crust of black flies creeps and quivers. A flurry of dirty water comes flooding down as I watch, and the flies rise in a stinking, humming mass.

I step back hurriedly to avoid them. A small shoe floats past me as the tide of filthy water ebbs and continues on down the hill. Something bigger moves in the drain and I see that it is a large frog.

I stand close against the wall of the house. Looking up, I notice a painted sign hanging from a bracket just above me. It depicts a loaf of bread and bears the words 'Job's Bakehouse'.

These houses look in terribly poor repair. Some have broken windows and a few window shutters are hanging loose. Dirt and rags are piled up against some of the walls. A trickle of sewage emerges from one of the alleys.

Suddenly I hear screaming. I look across the road in the direction from which it seems to be coming. A window in one of the houses flies open. A woman in middle age, her wispy dark hair falling wild and loose from under a white lace cap, hangs out of the window and, still screaming, looks up and down the street.

'Watchman! Watchman! You worthless toad! Where are you gone to?'

From behind her comes the sound of terrible groaning, so loud that I can hear it clearly over here. I find that I am trembling and cannot stop. I have heard that groaning before. I heard it earlier today on the stairs as I spoke to Mrs Bagling. So this world was right next to me even then. It was just waiting for me.

'Shiftless vermin!' The woman over the road seems literally to be trying to tear the hair from her head. She rips off her lace cap and slams it to and fro on the windowsill. Then from up the hill I hear footsteps approaching. They sound heavy as they suck and crunch on the slimy cobbles.

'Shut up, witch!' shouts a rough voice and the owner of the footsteps appears. He is a heavily built man in poor and dirty clothes, a long cloak wrapped round his shoulders. He is striding down the hill with an air of authority that looks as if he is not used to it. He is carrying in one hand a very large stick with a sharpened end, and in the other, a covered basket. This Red Riding Hood touch seems grotesquely inappropriate. 'I got your provisions, woman. Quit your howling!'

The woman is crying now and has vanished from the window. As the man reaches the house another man lurches out of a narrow alley near him. He also has a sharpened stick, this one with a glinting axehead fastened into it. He is rubbing his eyes and staggering. He is obviously drunk.

He moves out on to the cobbles and sways, staring blearily around. Neither of them has seen me yet, here in the shelter of the gable. I shrink back against the wall, keeping very still.

'Ungrateful bat,' the first man says to the drunken man. 'Some folks seem to reckon us watchmen are just their servants. But they're learning. They're learning.' He gives a quiet laugh and looks the other man up and down scornfully. 'Course, some of us takes our duties more seriously than others.'

The drunken man pushes his face forward, a pained attempt at concentration puckering his eyes. 'I'd like to know . . . whash . . . wha short of a man can wash . . . watch the folks he guards . . . dying by the thoushands . . . and not take to drink. I'd like to know thash, I would . . . like to know. Twould be a man of shtone, thas would. And thash . . .' He aims a smack at the face of the first man. 'Thash whash you are, James Bell, tash wosh you are . . .' He falls down on the cobbles.

The first man sighs, picks him up and props him against another of the doors bearing the red cross.

'Do your duty and save your blows for them as tries to escape, Edmund Lister, and heaven help my poor sister for being married to you.' He looks up at the house from which the woman's weeping can still be heard, and shouts, 'Come and get it then, witch!'

The woman reappears at a downstairs window. She is weeping hysterically now. ''Tis too late for my sister, watchman, for she is gone. Her pains are over, at last.' Sobs shake the woman so much that she can scarcely support herself with her hands leaning on the little high sill. 'I thank you anyway, watchman, for bringing us bread. You had better call for the examiners or chirurgeons, for my sister must be seen before the dead cart comes round tonight.'

'Dead cart'll be here afore the examiners,' mumbles the drunken watchman. 'There's many as dies uncounted, these days.'

The first watchman hands the basket up to the woman. 'I'm right sorry, lady,' he mutters.

The woman pulls the basket in then looks back down at the watchman, tears streaming down her face.

'And I'm right sorry,' she says more quietly now, 'that I tried to kill you, watchman.' She shakes her head from side to side. 'It was just our great need to escape . . . after our father died, to be shut up for forty days, it seemed beyond bearing, when neither of us had the signs nor tokens of the disease . . .'

The watchman lowers his stick and puts his hand to his neck. 'Aye well, lady, the gunpowder burns are healing now. I'll send for the examiners to certify your sister's cause of death.' He looks all round the street and then he sees me.

'You! Beggar!' He wags a finger at me. 'You know you

shouldn't be on the streets. Go down to the presbytery and fetch the examiners of health for me, or a chirurgeon or searcher will do, and I'll not hand you in.'

I glance to one side, to where a small alley runs beside the house. I must escape, but where will this alley lead me? It is in the same place as the alley which runs next to my own house, and down which I walk to school. The man approaches me, and at the same moment a thin woman sidles out of the alley.

'I'll go, watchman, for a farthing,' she whimpers in a weak voice. I recognise her. It is the ragged woman beggar who tried to protect me from Matchlock. She is so thin that she seems to be made of hunger. She clutches a ragged cloak round her and looks at me from black-ringed eyes, taking in my dress, my hair, my huddled stance by the wall. 'You're still on the streets then, lass. Yonder fancy law student didn't help you much, after all.' She glances up at the house. 'Best come with me. Otherwise the likes of Matchlock will surely get you.'

'No, I . . .'

The watchman approaches us and stands with his hands on his hips. Out of the corner of my eye I see the other watchman slide down the door and tip forward on to his face.

'Well, one of you fine ladies go, if you please. The dead may have to wait for Judgement Day but I don't see why they should wait for the examiners too.' He looks up at the sky. The last rim of the sun has gone and twilight is deepening. 'Another hour and the dead carts'll be on the streets.' He glances up at the notice that says 'Job's Bakehouse'. 'Thank the Lord the bakehouse's forty days are up tonight and we can get bread close by again.'

The drunken watchman over the road hauls himself into a sitting position, swaying like an unsteady toddler.

'Aye, unless another of them has taken the distemper since.'

The first watchman shakes his head. 'Nay, he's told me through the window. Only Job's wife Sarah took it. The rest of 'em stayed free. Almost a miracle it were. I'd have thought they'd escaped the back way or over the rooftops like plenty others, if it were not that I'd seen them at the windows.' He inhales deeply. 'Just smell that fresh bread baking. Enough to make you weep, it is. There'll be new loaves in the street by morn.'

From lower down the hill comes the sound of voices.

'Nightwatch is coming.' The drunken watchman tries to struggle to his feet. 'I'll be right thankful to get home.'

'God help us.' It is the woman at the window again. 'Master Watchman, I pray you stop gossiping with those trollops and fetch the examiners, for I swear the nightwatch will demand money for the service, and then dawdle and bring them too late. He is first cousin to the devil, that one, and he laughs at our infirmities.'

'Aye, I'd not wish Smiling Reuben on anyone, and I fear he has just arrived.' The first watchman flinches as he sees the group coming into view. His fear communicates itself to me. I wonder, with a prickle of trepidation, what can possibly be worse than the things I have seen already.

Twenty-three

THE GROUP CONSISTS OF TWO WELL DRESSED men holding small cloth bags to their noses and long red sticks out in front of them. The red sticks I recognise. They are the same as the one I saw in the hands of the bearer who stumbled along behind the dead cart. I realise that this must be a sign carried by officials whose job takes them into infected households. From time to time they wave the little cloth bags in front of them, as if to clear the air, and the strong smell of aromatic herbs reaches me.

Behind them come two men in rags, but recognisable as watchmen by their large, sharpened sticks. The first of these two watchmen is a stooped man with a button nose and close-set dark eyes. He has an unwavering, clown-like smile on his face, and his teeth are few and blackened.

'Oooh, lady beggars,' he coos, and comes straight up to me. His smile widens as he takes hold of my sleeve and pulls it sharply. The thin cotton rips. Outraged and frightened, I move hastily to one side to escape from him but he blocks my path.

'Such fancy rags.' He stares at my purple and lilac dress with its tie-dyed layers, then at my uncovered hair tightly up in its bun. 'What a sight she is.' He laughs and looks round for approval. 'Dear me, 'tis scarcely decent.' He lifts his hand and unexpectedly tugs at my hair so that it comes out of its bun.

'Let them be,' calls the first watchman from across the road. 'They were off to fetch the examiners, but now that the examiners are here anyway, these two can be gone and we'll not trouble 'em.'

'Ooooh, but speak for yourself.' The man, who must be Smiling Reuben, turns his attention to my companion, and taps her head with the blunt end of his stick. 'So, 'tis my friend Rachel again. The constables and deputies chose to let you off lightly, I gather. All my good work wasted, eh?'

'Come with me, lass,' the beggar woman mutters to me, and twisting sharply past him, she starts to run down the hill. I stand still. I want to run, but I am afraid that if I leave this spot which represents the nearest I can get to my own home at the moment, and go off into the wild, unknowable streets of seventeenth century London, then I shall never be able to find my way back.

The two well dressed men cross to the bakehouse door, frowning.

'Enough of all this,' orders one of them. 'We are here to release the residents of the bakehouse from their forty days' confinement, if indeed all within are wholesome. Unbar the door, watchmen.'

Reluctantly my tormentor leaves me, and he and his companion approach the bakehouse door with the keys that the drunken day watchman hands them. That is when I truly come to understand the nature of the shutting up of houses. Two iron bolts and two giant padlocks have been secured on the outside so that the residents cannot escape. This has been a prison, and its occupants completely at the mercy of the watchmen to bring them whatever they might need.

''Tis a pity we are now so short of watchmen that one

has to guard two houses on opposite sides of the road, Master Foe,' mutters one of the examiners to the other as they watch the padlocks spring loose.

''Tis a pity we are now so short of examiners that we have to work such hours,' replies the other.

'Aye well, 'tis our duty. Fresh bread for the neighbourhood is a necessity and we must have all the bakehouses open that we can. It is on the orders of the aldermen and common councilmen to the Company of Master Bakers. Two enclosed families have escaped from this street alone, whilst watchmen were off getting bread for them from Cling Alley.'

They shake their heads, watching the smiling watchman draw the bolts.

'One, believe it or not, was the family of Lovage, the churchwarden up the hill,' continues the first examiner. 'They had a back window on to the alley and they all climbed out, armed to the teeth with swords and pistols, crept down the hill by way of the alleys and courtyards, stole a dead cart and horses that were resting by day, and galloped off into the countryside, threatening to shoot anyone who got in their way.'

The second examiner widens his eyes in disapproval. 'You'd think a churchwarden would know better.' He sniffs the air. 'My, but that smells good. Job's bread was always the best.'

That is Mrs Bagling's bread, I think to myself, but then I realise that it is not. The smell is wonderful, but it is different, with a tangy undertone that our bread does not have.

'Move away, beggar girl,' says the examiner who has been addressed as Master Foe. He smiles at me not unkindly. 'You must get out into the countryside, young woman, for you know you will be thrashed and driven through the streets if you remain in London. We cannot have beggars, not now, with the risk of spreading the contamination more . . .'

'But I . . .'

Behind me the door is open, and I can hear people weeping with joy inside, but I cannot see them because the smiling watchman has now grabbed hold of me again and is shaking me.

'Hear what he says? Hear what the gentleman says?' His breath smells terrible and the pores of his face are ingrained with dirt. I close my eyes tightly and try to scream, but his hand clamps across my mouth, and I understand then that no one will help me, because in my casual twentieth century clothes, to these people I am a beggar, and therefore have no rights.

It is my fury that gives me strength, I think. I sag so that I am a dead weight in the watchman's grip. He staggers, and as he does so I punch him in the throat and kick him hard in the shins with my Doc Martens.

With a howl of agony my attacker goes sprawling on to the cobbles. I see one of his few remaining teeth fly out of his mouth. I am about to run, but as I turn, another hand takes hold of my arm, a large, warm hand with a comforting grip.

'I will have you dismissed from your work for this, watchman,' says a voice that I know. I turn and see Seth. His hand on my arm pulls me into the bakehouse. 'I thank you for releasing us, Master Foe,' he says to the examiner. 'I pray you come in, and you shall see that we are all well.'

In response to the two examiners' incredulous glances at me he adds, 'This is my . . . cousin.' I hear that his voice is wobbly and uncertain, and I realise that he is as confused as I am. It is one thing to ask a character in your dreams to come with you, but quite another when she really turns up on your doorstep.

'My . . . er . . . Cousin Emily has . . . fallen on hard times,' he continues. 'She has been far away in . . . the north country, and is quite free from contagion. She has had to wait a long time to visit me.'

Master Foe and the other examiner give me slight bows.

'Your pardon, mistress.'

I give a small curtsey, finding that the gesture comes quite naturally, and somehow knowing it to be correct.

'We would have brought a nurse searcher had we known there was to be a female in the house,' comments Master Foe. He turns back towards the street. 'Watchman! Fetch that beggar woman back. She looked decent enough. We will appoint her as nurse searcher. She's better than many we are forced to appoint in these sickly times. Get a move on, man. You owe her a favour.'

The fallen watchman picks himself up from the cobbles, dabbing with his hand at his mouth. He directs an expression of absolute hatred towards me, then he sets off down the hill at a run.

Master Foe sighs and watches him go. 'I declare, I do not know what we should do to fill the posts of bearers, buriers, nurses and watchmen, if there were not so many poverty-stricken people on the streets who will do anything at all to earn a farthing.'

'What about the beggar woman? Who shall check her for signs and tokens of disease, if she is to come into the house?' asks the second examiner under his breath.

Master Foe shrugs. 'She must check the girl and the girl must check her and they must both swear on the Good Book to be true in their declarations.'

The two men nod in agreement. I hear screams from down the hill and assume that the watchman has now found Rachel, the beggar woman. The door to the bakehouse stands open and the smell wafts out like a

—— 145 ——

promise of hope. Seth turns to me as he leads the way into the downstairs room. 'Greetings, cousin, and well met,' he says loudly for the benefit of the others. 'We have had a long wait for this moment, have we not?'

I nod, too overwhelmed by the situation to speak. Then, as the watchman arrives dragging the beggar woman, and as all the people mill about in the huge, low bakeroom, Seth turns to me and his composure is gone too.

'You actually . . . came . . . I don't understand it. How . . . ?' He runs his hands over my shoulders as if to check that I truly exist. 'I can scarce credit it. Are you . . . a ghost?'

I cannot answer him. I do not know any more what I am, or what he is, or anything at all about this terrifying world to which I have come.

Twenty-four

'I DO NOT RELISH THIS GIFT OF MINE, THIS terrible gift, of forward sight.' Seth is speaking very quietly so that Job will not hear. We are sitting by the fire in the bakehouse's downstairs room. The huge hearth, large enough to stand in, is disconcertingly in the same position as our own hearth, although nothing else about the room is the same.

I remember the estate agent saying that she thought parts of our hearth were the original Elizabethan construction, and I wonder if this is what I am seeing now, a hearth so solid that parts of it remained standing after the house that surrounded it fell into ruins, and which eventually formed the basis for the fireplace in the nineteenth century workman's cottage that took its place and in which we now live.

I have a sudden vision of the flowing of time, of time flowing both ways sometimes, like a river that runs upstream when the tide comes in. I have a vision of the things that float to and fro on a tide, people, man-made things, dangerous substances and forces, the rampant feelings of those in danger or extremity, tossed about, surfacing, vanishing and resurfacing.

This hearth has a blackened pot hanging over the flames and many more grouped around on trivets and suspended from hooks. They are crusted with the remains of ancient soups and stews round their rims, and feathered underneath with loose coatings of soot. There are brick ovens let into the wall all round the hot, smoky central fire. The heat is intense.

'In summer I use the ovens out the back,' Job tells me, leaning over to refill his mug of mulled ale from the large jug standing in the hearth, 'but when the weather turns a bit cooler it's good to have a nice bit of heat in the house.'

'Indeed.' I am picking up this way of talking. He's right about the heat. I smile weakly and wipe the sweat from my brow.

'They reckon the smoke keeps the contagion away too,' he adds. 'I throw juniper and wormwood, rosemary and rue on the fire, and I reckon that's what has kept the rest of us free from the distemper. Some folks go even further. Maybe you've heard of Solomon Eagle who goes round the streets with a great tray of burning charcoal on his head.'

'Still, he hasn't gone down with the plague yet, has he?' Seth grins.

Job gives him a withering look and turns back to me. 'Being from up north you won't know it, but we've had great bonfires lit all along the streets of London to try and stop the spread of the plague. Not that they've helped much.' He sighs. 'Aye, not that they've helped. It goes its own way and it seems nought can stop it. Perhaps the Lord in his wisdom has decided to destroy everyone in this sinful city.' He stamps away up the stairs, shaking his head.

I like Job. He is a big, curly-haired man, perhaps thirty years old, whose heat-flushed face shows the strain of the past days of imprisonment and the death of his wife. I have noticed tremors in his hands and tears in his eyes as he carries his great long-handled trays of loaves to and from the bread ovens. He has agreed to take on Rachel, the beggar woman, as bakehouse servant, and she is clearly overjoyed.

I look at Seth as he speaks to me haltingly and with many pauses. We have all been thoroughly checked for any signs of the round, black plague marks with inflamed edges, and for any indication of swellings, the plague buboes. We have all been pronounced clear and the examiners have gone away. The watchmen, however, are still outside the other houses in the street, and I am uncomfortably aware of the presence of Smiling Reuben with his sharpened stick and axehead, which I have now learnt is called a halberd.

'Why is there no watchman outside the third house on the other side of the road with the red cross on its door?' I asked Job earlier, when he had just finished chiselling the red writing off his own door.

He looked at me bleakly, moving round the room lighting candles in the sconces on the walls from a long taper. These are beeswax candles and they smell sweet.

'Because they're all dead, within, Mistress Emily. There is no one left to guard. They are all in the plague pit down the hill, and the house has been looted long since. There were fourteen in that house, three generations, and all took sick and died one after the other while their house was shut up for the first one, Master Andrew. I shall never forget their screams. It was pitiful. They were some of the first to go, in this part of London, but there have been many since.' He sighed and rubbed his face. The candles dipped and flickered as he paced round the room in a sudden surge of distress.

'How terrible.' I struggled to take in the scale of such suffering.

'I reckon that was where my Sarah picked up the illness,' Job went on, hoarsely. 'She was close friend to Elizabeth who lived there, wife of the eldest son. She came home from visiting them one day saying that

Elizabeth kept on about some sweet smell in the house, like mayflowers, and where could it be coming from, since the season of May was long gone. Course, at that time we weren't used to the symptoms of plague. Now everyone knows that mayflower is the smell of death. First the victim alone smells it, then it grows and grows until everyone can smell it, and it is so bad that all the posies and pouncet boxes in the world can scarce make it bearable for folks to come near the sufferer. You look shocked, mistress. Maybe you don't know all this, coming from up north where the Lord hasn't chosen to chastise you in this way, not like us city dwellers.'

He paused, and for a moment I thought the shock would kill me. A sick, choking feeling gripped me by the throat as I understood what had been happening to me before the chimney fell. And if this were so, if I did indeed have plague, back there in the time where I belonged, then I must find a way to return quickly to warn my family, before they too fell victim to it.

'Aye.' The baker sighed deeply and continued. 'It were a week later that Sarah sickened. Elizabeth was dead by then and all the rest were dying. Sarah fell into a terrible melancholia, as many do before the actual signs appear. She fought the illness though, and she lingered on for near a month, though mercifully she went into a deep sleep towards the end, and knew nothing.'

'They're the luckiest,' said Rachel, 'the ones that go into a deep coma.'

Deep . . . coma . . . For a moment the words seemed to have a strange echo to them. I looked round, puzzled by this sudden odd acoustic, but I could see no reason for it.

Job reached down a strange-looking pointed leather mask from a shelf. 'Seth and me, we had to wear these masks when we went near her, for protection. After she went mad, she thought we were monsters . . . Then after she was gone, Seth and me, we had to be shut up for another forty days, and her taken away on the dead cart, and no grave to visit. Aye, it's been hard . . .'

'Master Job . . .' I interrupted him. 'Master Job, can you tell me what the other symptoms of plague are? I fear . . .' I stood in front of him, weak with apprehension.

He took me by the arms and sat me down again. 'We all fear it, mistress. We all fear it. Here, have some garlic to tuck inside your cheek if you are affrighted. The symptoms? Well, there's a chill and a shivering. Folks feel dizzy and sick. They go off their food, and their heads pain them something terrible. Their hearts thud and they have a fearsome thirst. There's nose bleeds and mouth bleeds and sweating, then come the plague tokens, the black marks, sometimes purple or red, with their bright edges.'

He was clearly distressed by then and I wanted to stop him, but he ignored my attempts.

'How I detest that song the little brats used to sing,' he went on. 'It was so long since plague last hit London that they'd forgotten what it meant. "Ring-a-ring-a-roses, pocket full of posies". They don't sing it on street corners any more though.'

'They don't play out on street corners any more,' added Rachel. 'The only folks I've seen on street corners lately have been dead ones in heaps, when the bearers and buriers can't keep up.'

We all looked at her, appalled.

'I've heard the beggars singing that song, to taunt the rest of us,' said Job. 'Not you, of course,' he added hastily to Rachel.

Rachel shrugged. 'They get angry hearing people wail about being shut in. Most of them would be glad to have somewhere to be shut in, for 'tis far worse to be shut out.'

Job stared at her for a long moment, then he turned back to me and my question.

'Course, the last sign is the buboes, the swellings in the armpits and neck and thighs. Folks is more or less doomed then, unless the swellings burst or occasionally when the doctors cut or burn them open it can help, unless the victim dies of the remedy first.'

Suddenly tears started pouring down Job's cheeks. Seth interrupted here and tried to stop him.

'I think your dough in the hastener is risen and ready to go in the oven, Job,' he said. 'No point in going over old pains like this.'

Job was not to be silenced though, and all of us, Seth, Rachel and I, watched in dismay as he broke into sobs, howled out his anguish and smashed his hands repeatedly against the hot stones of the bread ovens. I was afraid he would smash his head against them too if we did not stop him, but he pushed me away and would not be comforted.

Twenty-five

MUCH AS I NEEDED TO TALK TO SETH, I COULD see it was necessary to listen to Job first. He talked for hours, in between kneading dough, mulling ale and hefting great trays of bread to and fro.

'Sarah near went mad with the pain,' he wept, slamming down a massive skein of dough on to the table. 'I tried to cut the swellings for her to let out the poison, but she cursed me and tried to set her bed alight with a candle. I hope and pray that she is not in hell for that.'

I found that I was in tears too.

'She was very brave for a long time,' put in Seth. 'She carried on teaching the lute even when she knew that taking people into the house was a risk. She was a good woman, Job.'

Job wasn't listening. 'Perhaps the Lord will forgive her because she went mad,' he whispered. 'Plenty do go mad, you know. They go running naked and screaming round the streets if they can escape from their confinement. I've seen two at different times go down Beggarsgate. They fling theirselves into the Thames to end it quicker. That is where I should be . . .' His voice dropped. 'I should like to go mad.' He said it almost pleadingly.

We all made efforts to soothe him, but he only became more and more distressed, and I realised then that this anguish had been stored for too long, and that it had to come out, and if one man felt like this, then the total of all the agony across this city might have been enough to print it for ever on the air we breathe and the ground we walk.

Job went on mumbling and weeping and Seth tried to persuade him to go to bed, but he said he must finish baking his bread.

As he lifted the last tray of risen dough from the hastening oven to the baking oven he told us how the final plague sufferer left alive in the now-deserted house over the road, Mistress Tilly, the grandmother, had climbed out of her garret window, four storeys up, made her way over the rooftops to avoid the watchmen, then run down the hill and thrown herself into the plague pit after the dead cart took the last of her grandchildren there. When she refused to get out, the bearers and buriers dragged her out with long hooks before the next lot of corpses could fall on her, but they found that she had died whilst she lay there.

'Buried herself,' said Job. 'Buried herself, she did.' He wiped his eyes on his apron. 'When I was a child I remember Mistress Tilly was always saying, "If you want a job done properly, do it yourself . . ."' He went and stood facing the front window where the statutory single candle burned. 'So she did it herself, she did. Buried herself, she did.'

Rachel, who had been refilling Job's mug of ale regularly, clearly ecstatic with joy at being able to serve this person who had given her work and a roof over her head, now took it away from him. She stood next to him for a moment, also staring at the window, though nothing could be seen but their candlelit reflections, fragmented against the tiny dark panes.

''Tis terrible to see the candles in the windows grow fewer every night,' Rachel commented. 'We notice it, out there on the streets. It is as if the whole world is gradually being snuffed out.'

Job glanced at Rachel, then stared more intently at her, and frowned.

'Strange . . .' He shook his head. 'It is strange how being shut in . . . can make a person unable to tell dreams from reality . . . Do I know you, madam? I feel as if I have dreamt about you sometime.'

Rachel lowered her eyes. 'I have seen you here and there, sir. You have doubtless also seen me, though you may not remember it.'

I went and stood near them. There were no curtains at this window, and the darkness outside seemed threatening and very close. I am aware of it still now, as I sit talking to Seth, trying to make sense of this situation in which we find ourselves.

Job has found clothes for both Rachel and myself from the wardrobes of his dead wife, Sarah. They are very short and loose on me, and I feel very awkward wearing them with poor Sarah so recently in her grave, but it is better than looking as out of place as I did before. Now Job is asleep in his chair by the fire and Rachel is heating a fresh jug of mulled ale by plunging a red hot poker into it. The liquid hisses fiercely and bubbles up the sides.

'So you knew it was forward sight?' I prompt Seth. 'You knew you were seeing the future?'

He takes a sip from his mug of ale, then reaches over and pours me some more.

'Not at first. No, I thought it was just dreams and nightmares. I only realised the truth when I saw the dates on your news sheets. They have such very fine printing in your time, much finer than in our *Intelligencer*, but nonetheless I thought at first that it must be a printing mistake. It took me a while, as the visions became clearer, to realise . . . to see how everything else fitted in . . . then I thought it was the work of devils . . .' He shakes his head. 'I thought I was being punished . . .'

I sip my ale. I must just let him talk. It seems to be a need of people who have been shut up for a long time. The drink is warm and spicy. My head swims. I drink some more. 'Punished, Seth? What for?'

He avoids my eyes and ignores my question. 'My Aunt Audrey had the forward sight, and it drove her mad in the end, they say. Certainly she was mad when I knew her as a child. I fear that will be my fate one day, Emily, to go mad from seeing the future . . .'

I want to tell him that seeing the past isn't much better either, but he is still talking in his fast, low voice, rolling his painted earthenware mug between his palms and staring down into the steam.

'I think the terror of enclosure may have caused it — I don't know. Perhaps the mind escapes when the body cannot. You cannot imagine the desperation to get out — to get out and go anywhere, by any means. Of course, madness is on everyone's minds, with the illness driving so many out of their senses, and that is what I thought was happening to me when the dreams and visions started.'

I want to say to him that perhaps it is my own stress and misery too that has similarly caused me to be a vehicle for this strange process of movement through time, but there is something else that I must ask him first.

'And what about Pardoner?'

I am totally unprepared for his reaction.

'Pardoner!' He spills some of his ale on to the floor. 'What do you know about Pardoner?'

I am flabbergasted. 'Well, you told me about him. You were looking for him, you know, when you were in my house . . .'

'In your house? I have never been in your house! How can you know of these things? Are you a witch? Please don't speak to me of Pardoner, for Pardoner is dead. He is dead! Do you understand me?'

I stand up and back away. I feel abruptly that I do not know Seth at all, as indeed I do not, and I must have been mad ever to think that I did.

'Pardoner is dead,' repeats Seth more calmly. 'I understood the necessity, the vile unspeakable necessity to destroy all the cats and dogs in London. It was painful, but I did understand, for they can spread the plague, or so the Justices of the Peace told us . . .'

'You killed him?' I am incredulous. 'You killed Pardoner?'

He shudders, then takes a great draught of his ale. Some of it dribbles down his chin. He wipes it on his sleeve. I cannot believe the calmness and reasonableness of his voice as he continues speaking of such terrible things.

'It was hard for people to lose their pets. Particularly for those shut up, with others outside unwilling to talk to them either, as if the black death could be spread even by words . . . Then not to have the animals who at least had always been there to listen and comfort . . .' He pauses and swallows. 'Pardoner was my friend. I did not have him long but I shall never forget him.'

'You killed him?' I repeat, stupidly. Seth looks away and does not answer me. I remember my dream, when I sleepwalked, of Seth with the lump of granite that dripped blood. Is that the awful secret of Jonah's room? Is that where Seth killed his cat?

I stare at him in horror, and suddenly I know that whatever the truth is, good or evil, I do not trust Seth at all.

Twenty-six

NOW I REALLY DO NOT UNDERSTAND. I WONDER if Seth is actually mad already, like his Aunt Audrey. Or is he just drunk? One thing I am sure of is that he is lying.

He was grief-stricken for his cat when I first met him. Now he is shifty and not that bothered. I think again about the conclusion I came to on Saturday night, that I was probably seeing the past in the wrong order. Now I have entered it at a certain point and must be seeing it in the right order. Perhaps some of the things I saw before have not yet happened.

I want to question Seth, but I hesitate. His anger was alarming. I remember what seemed to be his admission of murder on the night I caught him in our house. Whom did he murder? Could that murder maybe not have happened yet? This is a frightening thought. Or was he referring to the killing of his cat?

I put my drink down on the table and try to frame a question. Job has woken up and he sees me struggling for words.

'I daresay you have as much of a problem with our southern speech as we do with your strange northern talk, Mistress Emily,' he comments. I smile at him, and am about to agree, but at that moment I hear the distant sound of a bell. I know it now. It is the dead cart. Gradually a gruff voice becomes audible.

'Bring our your dead! Bring out your dead!'

I cross to the door and open it a crack and peer out, and in the few moments before Seth seizes the door from me and slams it shut, I see once again the terrible sight of the large flat cart approaching, pulled by two horses and piled high with bodies. This time the linksman carries a lantern. The cart stops at the house opposite, where the watchman has unlocked the padlock on the door and drawn back the bolts. A body is brought out wrapped in cloths, and thrown on top of the heap.

'Oh,' I gasp. 'How terrible.'

The crash of that door shutting is echoed by our own. Seth latches and bolts it firmly, then abruptly he puts his arms round me and rocks me for a moment against the rough lace of his shirt.

'Indeed, it is a sorry thing when there are no funerals any more, and no wood for coffins, and all souls go nameless into the earth together, many with none left to mourn them.'

We are all silent for a moment, then Job hands me a candle in an engraved silver holder and says, 'Best get to bed, Mistress Emily. Seth will show you to your room. Rachel, you can sleep in the cubby behind the hearth. 'Twill be right cosy for you there.'

Rachel wipes her perspiring face on her apron and nods with touching thankfulness. I follow Seth up the stairs. We both carry candles in matching candlesticks. The candlelight gleams on their delicate silver traceries and throws into emphasis the rough-plastered walls on either side of us.

Here I start seeing similarities to our own house. The stairs follow a bend in the same way, although they are steeper and much narrower. At the top, Seth's room is more or less in the same position that Jonah's room would have been, and mine is almost where my real room would be. Seth gestures to the closed wooden door of my room and turns away. For a moment I am gripped by the idea that this might all be a dream, a product of my high temperature. If only it could be, I wish desperately. What am I doing here? How can I ever get back?

'Seth, I want to go home,' I whisper, and I find that I want to cry.

Seth looks down at me and narrows his eyes. I am suddenly forcibly aware of the three centuries that separate us.

'I daresay you will,' he says shortly. 'Indeed, I half doubt that you are here at all, even now.' He turns away but does not open the door to his own room. I wait. I feel a great need to see inside his room, and to find out if it contains whatever horror Jonah's room also contains. I loiter on the landing.

'Have you lodged here long, Seth?' This type of polite conversation seems ridiculous under the circumstances. Seth still makes no move to open his door.

He shrugs. 'A while. A year, ever since my law studies began.'

I wait. He surely can't keep the door shut for ever. 'And your parents? Where do they live?'

'Oh, far out of London in a tiny village called Knightsbridge. You will not have heard of it. Well, I expect you will wish to retire to bed now, Emily.' He opens my door for me. 'I hope you will be comfortable there.'

He moves to stand with his back to his own closed door and waits. Reluctantly, holding my candle far out in front of me, I enter my room. It is unfurnished except for a small straw mattress on a wooden truckle in a corner, and a low chest of the same type as the Restoration coffer, though smaller.

I leave the door ajar, and after a few moments I hear

Seth's latch click. Quickly I step back out on to the landing, but he is too fast for me. His door has already closed with him inside. In frustration I cross the landing and listen with my ear at his door, and the sound that I hear then makes me understand everything.

Twenty-seven

*T*HERE'S NO POINT IN GIVING HIM TIME FOR concealment. I just walk straight in. He could hardly be undressed yet, but even if he was, I couldn't care less. Seth has deceived me, but I can fully understand why.

As the door swings open there is a horrified gasp at one side of the room and a scrabbling flurry of movement at the other. Seth stands with a small dish in his hand. Pardoner, whose mewing I heard from outside, frisks into the air then rushes towards me.

I push the door hurriedly shut behind me. Seth slams down the dish so that water splashes all over his shirt, then he advances on me fast with his hand raised. For a moment I think he is going to hit me, but instead he slams his hand against the door so that the latch clicks violently into place.

Then we both stand frozen for a moment, before Seth says quietly, 'How *dare* you!'

I bend to stroke his cat. I am not going to apologise. I look up and see rage and panic on Seth's face.

'You've managed to keep him hidden all this time?' I ask incredulously.

'Well, it would seem so, wouldn't it. Yes, I have kept him hidden ever since the order went out from the Lord Mayor and the Justices of the Peace for all dogs and cats to be slaughtered. Until now,' he says tightly.

'How . . . ? Didn't they check?'

He bends down and takes Pardoner away from my stroking hand. The little cat is purring loudly. It bats playfully at Seth's long hair as he holds it up against his cheek.

'Oh yes, they checked, but before the official exterminators came round I killed a large rat — very messily — you couldn't tell what it had been when I had finished with it. It was the same colour as Pardoner and the same size — even Sarah and Job were deceived. I showed it to the exterminators and then I wept a lot, and buried it at the back behind the outside bread ovens. Sarah and Job comforted me and I put on quite a show of grief. That was the worst part of all the deception. The rest was relatively easy. I have a secret cavity in the wall that Pardoner loves in hide in . . .'

He turns away and goes and sits on the bed and looks at me silently.

'It's all right . . .' I speak gently to Seth as if I were speaking to the cat itself. 'I won't give you away. If Pardoner had been carrying the plague fleas you would have been dead by now.'

'Fleas? What are you talking about?'

Of course, they didn't know.

I cross the room and sit down next to Seth. Pardoner has wriggled free and is jumping about on the bed. I put my hand out and stroke the cat's plush head, and as I do so I realise to my amazement that although the tiny animal is as always very thin, there is no sign of any injury to its head. I frown. This is very strange. I feel the beginnings of disquiet.

Seth is still staring closely at me. His face shows the tension of the past months.

'It must have been very difficult and worrying,' I say quietly.

He reaches out his hand to the cat but then instead takes hold of my hand. 'It was worrying but not truly so difficult. Job hardly ever comes up here, for fear of disturbing my studies — I rent the whole of this floor, you understand — and poor Sarah was too ill . . .'

But something has happened. It is as if the contact of Seth's hand has woken me from a trance. I look round the room, at the bed, the table, the bench and the chair. Seth's expression changes and he releases my hand.

'What is it? What is the matter, Emily?'

'Dear Lord . . .'

'Emily, what *is* it? What . . . can you see? Is it a vision? I have seen visions in this room . . .'

'No . . . No, it is . . . the room.'

The room is the same. It is the same as the room in my sleepwalking dream. I did not realise while my attention was focused on Pardoner and then on Seth's anger at me, but now I see it. The cupboard and stool, the carved chair and wooden bed with its soft, cream blankets, the small high window casting a rainbow radiance on to the wall, Seth in *these clothes*.

I stand up but my knees are shaking so I have to sit down again. If the room is real, then the dream was also real. I see again vividly the green granite doorstop, the blood dripping, the look of absolute despair on Seth's face.

'Seth, you've got to get out of here.' I speak very fast. 'Now. Just go. Don't ask me why. You must just go, please. Escape.'

'What? I don't understand you, Emily. What are you talking about? Why should I go? I am safer here than anywhere . . .'

There comes the sound of a sudden loud commotion downstairs, someone hammering at the front door and a voice shouting. The voice is slurred, masculine with high inflections, and I recognise it. It is the voice of the watchman who attacked me, Smiling Reuben. 'Bread!' it shouts. 'I seek penny loaves from the baker and his slatterns!'

Seth crosses quietly to his door and slides the bolt. 'It's what I should have done before *you* got in,' he says drily. 'Don't worry. People have heard that the bakehouse is open again. Job often used to get drunkards calling at all hours of the night when they smelt the bread, but he never lets them in. He's too drunk himself at the moment, anyway.'

The hammering increases, then there is an explosive crash of breaking glass. Quickly Seth strides to the side of the room opposite the door and to my astonishment pulls out a section of wall. The solid plaster with a cross-hatching of twigs behind it comes out to reveal a cavity in the hollow wall.

Outside the door, I hear footsteps coming up the stairs at a run. 'Sir! Sir!' It is Rachel's voice. 'What shall I do? I cannot wake the master.' She taps on the door.

Rapidly Seth scoops Pardoner up and puts him into the hollow wall on a little bed of straw and wool that I glimpse there, then he rams the plaster back into place and opens the door.

'Oh, sir.' Rachel glances beyond him to me but seems unsurprised to see me there. 'I did not know what to do. Master Job cannot be roused so I have let the customer in, but I do not know what to charge him for the loaves. He has a smashed bottle with him, sir, and he does not look inclined to pay at all . . .'

'You let him *in*?' exclaims Seth incredulously. 'Lord preserve us, Rachel, but you have a lot to learn. It's all right. I shall come down and let him out again. As for the price of bread, do you think it likely that a penny loaf might cost a penny?'

I feel sorry for Rachel and annoyed at Seth for his sarcasm towards her, but infinitely relieved that he is going down to deal with the watchman.

There is something wrong though. Heavy footsteps are coming up the stairs, fumbling stumbling footsteps. Seth goes out on to the landing and I peer out past him, holding out the silver candlestick in front of me. A terrible reek of ale rolls up the stairwell and a dark figure is lurching to and fro, propping itself from wall to wall on the narrow steps.

'There she is, the beggar girl!' He has seen me in the flickering light. 'It's you I've come for!' he shouts at me, the clown-smile remaining grotesquely on his face whilst his button eyes are full of hatred. I recoil back into the room and put my candlestick down, looking round for some means of protection. I think longingly of the goat-headed poker in my own house. Then I see the doorstop. It is behind the door, tucked into a corner. Its ridged, grey-green surface is webbed and dusty with lack of use.

Outside the room I hear Seth's raised voice then the sound of scuffling. I pick up the doorstop. Rachel backs across the room, an expression of terror on her face.

'He is a very devil, that watchman,' she whispers as she wraps her arms around herself and presses her back against the far wall. There is a crack as the section of plaster concealing Pardoner tilts to one side behind her. With a mewing chirrup of delight the little cat flounces out into the room.

'Oh no!' I reach out to catch the cat but he is frightened and runs round the room in a frenzy. Rachel stares at him in astounded disbelief.

'A cat!' she whispers.

'Look after him,' I say to her sharply. I feel I must get to Seth and help him. I heft the doorstop in my two hands but at that moment there is a howl and a groan from outside and the door flies open and hits me. I am knocked to the floor and the heavy doorstop falls from my hands. I stagger back to my feet just in time to see the watchman bring his broken bottle down on Seth's head.

For a moment, everything goes very quiet. Seth lies motionless on the floorboards. Rachel and I move round the edge of the room towards each other. The watchman stands looking down at what he has done.

Then he sees the cat. For a moment his smile falters with surprise then it widens even more than ever. He closes the door and picks up the doorstop. The candle flames billow with the movement. Shadows swoop all round the room.

'Time for a reckoning,' says the watchman. He runs a finger over his few tombstone teeth, then touches the heavy end of the doorstop with a little kissing sound.

'The lady beggars can wait. First I have to deal with a nasty little crime, the sort of crime that makes my job all the harder because it puts others in danger. The crime of concealing a cat.'

With a shockingly fast movement the watchman lunges across the room and snatches Pardoner from where he is now cowering under the table by the wall. I move, but not fast enough. He has the animal by the neck, and with his other hand he whirls the doorstop in a great circle and smashes it down on Pardoner's head.

Twenty-eight

I SEE THE ARC OF BLOOD ON THE WALL, IN THE place where one day Jonah's chest of drawers will stand. I see Pardoner scuttering and dragging himself crablike towards the stairs in the semi-darkness. I see Seth stumble to his feet and seize the doorstop from the watchman and raise it above his head. I see, in shock, Rachel drawing a sword from among Seth's clothes hanging on the back of the door. It is astonishing how much you can see in just one blink of an eye.

Then I have grabbed one of the silver candlesticks and I am running after the cat. The candle goes out with the draught of air on the stairs. I trip and stumble and finally turn the bend and reach the bottom where the fire in the hearth still throws out warmth and light. I look round desperately for Pardoner. The front door stands wide open and he is nowhere to be seen.

'Sarah? Sarah?' It is Job, tottering out from his room at the back of the bakehouse. He stares around him in confusion. He is very drunk still. I look past him into his room, searching for the cat, and I see there, next to the bed, a beautiful carved chair with red velvet cushions and a fringed back — our chair. Near it, propped against the wall, stands a curved-backed stringed instrument, Sarah's lute. A small painting hangs on the wall. It is of a woman, and I realise that this is the woman from my first dream, and also the lute player from the television.

Then I look at Job in profile and I know him too, more worn and tired and sad now, more plainly dressed, but the same man who sang 'Greensleeves'.

'Greensleeves,' I whisper, and with a yearning look of drunken dependence in his eyes, Job starts to sing it in a high, soft voice, tears rolling down his cheeks. The pure, beautiful sound echoes round the house, backed by the noise of strife from upstairs, while I rush frantically from room to room searching for the cat. When I do not find him I go to the front door and stand on the dark threshold and look up and down the impenetrable street.

'Pardoner?' I call. 'Pardoner?'

'Oh *Pardoner*,' mimics a voice from the shadows. '*Pardoner*,' and it is like last time, but the voice has become a terrible thing now, a depths of the night, depths of the pit voice, the voice of disease, from within the alley next to the house. Then Matchlock comes storming out of the darkness, arms flailing.

I have less than a second in which I see him facing me, framed against the bakehouse doorway, as I reel back in horror. He is bare-chested still. On his skin are circular black marks with wet, puckered red edges, far larger than when I last saw him. His arms are raised like a scarecrow's, because the size of the swellings beneath them prevents him from lowering them.

These plague buboes look hard, white and shiny, one of them leaking pus and blood. Matchlock's head is tilted sideways, like that of a broken doll, by another such swelling in his neck. His eyes have almost disappeared into a welter of red inflammation.

I stare at him with pity. I crave the power to help him, to pluck this desperate man out of history and transfer him to a twentieth century hospital with antibiotics and starched nurses who would not stand for any of his nonsense.

'Water,' he gasps. 'Give me water.' I see that his mouth is raw with sores. He coughs, and blood jumps on to his lip.

'Yes.' I turn to find where the water is kept. 'I'll get you water. Wait. I just have to find it . . .'

'Water! Water!' he repeats. 'Where has all the water gone? Rain and sleet and candleleet and Christ receive my soul . . .'

Two things happen simultaneously. From the corner of my eye I see Pardoner edging his way tentatively out of one of the bread ovens. At the same moment Matchlock emits a great, swelling roar and comes crashing into the house straight at me. With one of his scarecrow arms he slams me back against the door jamb. My teeth clap together and I bite my tongue. The back of my head cracks against the worn grey oak of the timber framing, and I slide down, feeling the splintery roughness on the side of my neck.

The room whirls and goes distant. 'Greensleeves' resonates in my head. Helpless, and as if from far off, I see Pardoner go limping and blundering out of the door, and The Plague come marching in.

Antibiotics. Antibiotics, the word is jangling in my brain to the tune of 'Greensleeves', but someone else seems to be saying it.

'You need antibiotics, Matchlock,' I say.

'They're working, Mrs Strachan. Her fever's down.'

'But she still seems to be delirious.'

'No, I don't think so. She's just dreaming. She sleepwalked last night when you went home for that couple of hours. Did doctor tell you?'

'No.' It's Mum's voice. 'No, but she often does sleepwalk at home.'

I open my eyes. Mum and a nurse are watching me, their faces disconcertingly close. The nurse is a plump woman with a starched white cap. Both of them are wearing surgical masks over their faces. The nurse is holding my wrist, taking my pulse. I can feel its thud, thud, thud in my head as I am reunited with my headache. I become aware of a soreness on my cheek where the brick grazed it. My neck hurts too, but this is more recent, more painful, from where I slid down the timber framing of Job's bakehouse.

Mum smiles. 'Hello darling. How are you feeling? What a fright you've given us this past week.' She strokes my cheek.

I cannot smile back. All around me stand the invisible figures of Seth, Rachel, Job and Matchlock, and over me hangs the grinning face of the murderous watchman.

'Mum . . .'

'Yes darling?'

My voice croaks with lack of use. My mouth feels full of sores and my tongue seems swollen. 'Mum, where's Pardoner?'

'He's at home. I'm keeping him in because he's had his vaccinations and they seem to have made him jumpy.'

'Is he all right?'

'Yes of course. He's doing fine. Dad's here, Em. Would you like him to come in and see you?'

'Yes, but Mum, what's the matter with me? Am I in hospital?' I swivel my eyes to look round the room. My neck is too sore to turn my head. The lights are quite dim but they are still hurting my eyes. My left eye feels sore and crusty and hard to open properly.

Mum and the nurse glance at each other.

'Well dear,' says the nurse, whose name badge says Sister Alcibiades, 'you came in here because part of a chimney fell on you, but then I'm afraid we found you had something rather worse than a knock on the head wrong with you. Try not to get upset, but you're suffering from bubonic plague.'

I nod. 'Oh . . . yes.'

The nurse and my mother glance at each other again, approvingly.

'She's taking it very well,' says Mum.

'A very sensible girl.' The nurse lets go of my wrist. 'One or two of our isolation patients have panicked when they realised what they had got.' She bends over me again, speaking clearly as if to a deaf and elderly person. 'You've been on the television and in the newspapers, dear. "Schoolgirl is latest victim of museum plague contact", it said.' She smiles. 'Nice to be famous for something, eh?'

'How many people have plague, then?' I ask, moving about to try and make my aching back and limbs more comfortable.

Sister Alcibiades adjusts my pillows and thinks for a moment. 'It'll be twenty now, with Mrs Bagling. Alice Smith is going home today, and there shouldn't be any more. They're keeping a close watch at the airports, and monitoring people who have been on holiday to India.'

She sighs. 'You think of these great health scourges as things of the past, but it just goes to show.' She shakes her head and moves away towards the door. 'We always have to be vigilant. These things can never truly be said to be past.'

It seems I was unconscious and delirious for nearly a week. I am in hospital for another ten days. My temperature rises and falls and I am told it has been as high as forty-one degrees Celsius. I suffer from stomach pains and vomiting. I have prolonged coughing fits and sometimes feel as if I am suffocating. I have several nosebleeds and am reminded of the rats I saw dying on Hound Hill.

People visiting me wear white face masks, light surgical ones, totally unlike the heavy pointed leather monster masks with eyeholes that had so frightened poor Sarah. They come in twos, Mum and Roger, Dad and Jonah, both sets of grandparents bearing sweets and chocolates, Great Grandmother Strachan all the way from Cumbria, Miss Patel still demanding homework from Matthew Rodriguez, a few other people from school, Samantha and Rose.

These two stay for almost a whole afternoon, and when they are finally ejected by Sister Alcibiades, Rose says, 'Oh well, come on then Sammicakes,' and Samantha and I exchange an amused and wordless look. I know then that something important to me has been restored, and perhaps had never been lost in the first place, except through the faulty lens of my own misery.

Sister Alcibiades says my illness doesn't seem to have turned pneumonic, but the face masks are a precaution, since the doctors are rather mystified as to how I managed to contract the bubonic form of the disease in the first place. The museum and Alice Smith's flat have been fumigated just in case some plague-bearing fleas were brought home in Alice's luggage.

I am given several large injections of antibiotics every day from huge syringes. I come to dread them. I find that I have a grotesque swelling on the side of my neck that has the hardness and consistency of a leather football, and that it is this which is causing my neck pain and not the graze from Job's door jamb.

'I look like a monster,' I say to Jonah.

He smiles in agreement. Gradually the swelling goes down as the days drag by.

On the morning that I go home there is a panic on in the hospital because the drugs department has been burgled.

'What a time to lose every gram of tetracycline and streptomycin that we possess,' frets Sister Alcibiades to my mother as she brings my prescription back from the dispensary. 'You'll have to go to your own chemist for this. I'm sorry.'

At home, great black tarpaulins cover most of the roof. I go up the stairs in wonderment to look at Jonah's room. He is staying at Matthew's until his room is repaired. All his furniture is crammed into my room and I can only get in there with difficulty.

'Sorry about this,' says Mum. 'There was nowhere else to put it.'

I stand on the threshold of Jonah's room and look at the hole in the roof where the chimney fell in. The black plastic covering the hole shifts and sighs. Most of the debris has been cleared away and there are signs of the rebuilding work that has started. A ladder and some wooden beams lie by the wall. There is dust everywhere.

I look at the far wall. The chest of drawers has gone and the wall has marks where it was gouged by falling tiles. Standing here, I cannot believe that Seth is not somewhere near. I try to step forward but at once the old fear grips me. I stare at the spot where Pardoner's blood hit the wall. As I do so I feel again the evil of the smiling watchman as clearly as if he were behind me. I turn quickly, but there is no one there.

'Emily!' Mum calls up the stairs. 'Time for your tablets. Can you come down please?'

I stand for a moment more. Before I go I whisper under my breath, 'Seth?'

There is no reply.

Twenty-nine

'T HE MEMBERS OF THE BEGGARSGATE GROUP are very anxious to see you again,' says Roger, while Mum is driving Great Grandmother Strachan to the station to start her journey home. It is about a week after my return from hospital. Mrs Bagling, paler and quieter, is now back home too.

'Oh?'

'Are you well enough to come to a meeting tomorrow night?'

I stroke Pardoner as he sleeps on my lap by the fire. I am overwhelmed by how good it is to be back home. I don't want to think about the Beggarsgate Group or about anything to do with the terrible history of this place. The fact that I have seen it with my own eyes, lived a few moments of it, is just a freak of nature, of time, a manifestation of things we don't understand, like clairvoyance or UFOs or water divining or corn circles. I can live with that. I have escaped from Matchlock and Smiling Reuben and I must count myself lucky.

I look down at the sleeping, purring cat. He is lying on his back with all his feet in the air. Pardoner has escaped, too. He has escaped across the centuries from an age that wanted to kill him. He is warm and content. I can still feel his bones through his fur, but he is gaining weight. Pardoner and I have seen terrible things and we will comfort each other and gradually the fear will recede and we will never ever go into Jonah's room.

'I'm sorry Roger, but I think I want to forget about the Beggarsgate Group.'

He looks stricken. 'But Emily . . . why? Has something happened? It has, hasn't it? You see . . .'

Mum comes back and Roger breaks off to go and make a pot of tea. Mum produces a plate of Mr Kipling jam tarts. For once there is no chocolate cake. I take this to be a sign of something. Roger comes back and pours the tea.

'Sorry, I haven't had time to bake, but these are very nice,' says Mum. She looks completely unapologetic and sits down next to Roger.

I feel a twinge of disappointment. It had seemed a hopeful sign when she and Dad stood together at my bedside in the hospital, but the disappointment is only a twinge. I stretch out my feet toward the fire. It is billowing smoke into the room because the loss of a section of the main chimney, which this branch joins further up, is causing it not to draw properly. The telephone rings and Mum goes over to answer it.

'You see,' goes on Roger, 'the fact of the matter is that Alice Smith has disappeared. She never reached home after leaving the hospital. She got into a taxi and that was the last anyone saw of her. Miss Patel is very worried.'

'What does that have to do with me? I haven't even met her.'

Roger leans down and straightens the hearthrug. A magazine open at one of his poems is lying on the floor and he closes it and puts it neatly into the newspaper rack.

'The thing is, Emily, it was quite clear, even before Alice caught plague, that all she wanted to do was to go back to the past. She had lost all interest in the twentieth century. She didn't appear to mind the discomfort or disease. This person, the one we think she was involved

— 176 —

with back there, well . . . all I can say is that she seemed completely besotted . . .'

Roger starts straightening the tassels on the hearthrug. 'She was like you. She could see . . . more . . . than the rest of us in the Beggarsgate Group. It's just possible that you might come up with some clue, some idea, that might help. Her friends, particularly Miss Patel, really just want to know whether or not she's all right. Her closest relative is an aunt, and she has already reported Alice missing to the police.'

Mum comes back. 'That was Theodora Bagling. She's just heard on the local news that they've found some of Alice's clothing, a silk scarf and a floral waistcoat, in a drain up the hill. Doesn't sound too good, does it.'

I curl up in the chair and rub my chin to and fro across Pardoner's ears.

'All right,' I say quietly to Roger. 'I'll come to the meeting.'

As this is an unscheduled meeting of the Beggarsgate Group we go straight up the hill to the candle shop the following evening. The museum has anyway been sealed off by the health authorities.

It has been a cool afternoon, and now a fine, mothy rain is drifting in the light from the street lamps, giving them haloes like candles. Roger and I walk side by side, not speaking. The rain clings to our skin and hair and we are quite wet by the time we arrive.

In the back room the group are all there. Frances who owns the candle shop is talking to a young man in a tweed jacket.

'That's John who owns the antique shop,' says Roger. 'Come and meet him.'

We cross the room.

'I'm so pleased with the candlestick I bought from you yesterday,' Frances is saying to the young man. 'How did you say you came by it? Roger said there was some strange story.'

'Yes.' John frowns. 'A taxi driver brought it in to sell. He said someone he picked up gave it to him instead of paying her fare. That must be the most expensive taxi ride ever, considering that the candlestick is worth at least five hundred pounds and maybe more.'

'Well, it was good of you to let me have it for that.' Frances reaches up to where a beeswax candle burns on top of a bookshelf, and lifts down an engraved silver candlestick with a curved handle. 'Quite a beauty, isn't it.' She shows it round the room.

Roger nods admiringly. 'I wish I could have afforded it myself. Emily, this is John,' he continues, but then he looks at my face and stops. 'What?'

I reach out and take hold of the candlestick. The room falls silent as one by one people become aware of something unusual.

'What?' Frances repeats Roger's question.

I stroke the candlestick, cradle it. I try to remember where I put the other one after I came downstairs with it in Job's bakehouse, stumbling and falling in my dash to catch Pardoner. I stare into the polished silver with its fine tracery of herons and reeds.

I look at John and sit down. John sits down too. I hold the candlestick between us, staring into the candle flame.

'This candlestick . . . as far as I know . . . it was last used on this hill in a bakehouse that stood here in 1665. I can't think how it comes to be here now. You say it was used as a taxi fare, and Alice was last seen getting into a taxi?' I hesitate. My mind is churning. 'Then all I can think is that someone who had access to this candlestick . . . came back with it, to . . . collect her.'

I feel very tired. 'I'm sorry. I'm going home now. I may be wrong, but I think this almost certainly means that Alice has chosen to go back to the plague year. Someone came for her and she has . . . gone with them.'

Thirty

I FIND I DON'T WANT TO TELL THE BEGGARSGATE Group any more than just the bare fact that I have seen the Great Plague of London. Even my small experience of it was so terrible that words are inadequate. I sense their raging curiosity, but for now they accept my unwillingness to talk.

There doesn't seem much point in talking to Roger or to Matthew Rodriguez on the way home either. After Matthew has said a subdued good night and crossed the road to his house, I ask Roger, 'Are you going to marry my mother?' I really can't be bothered with polite conversation, but I feel as if I want to get matters in this century sorted out, even if other centuries remain completely out of control.

Roger looks surprised and hesitates. 'Well . . . we haven't really known each other very long, so it's hard to say, but I shouldn't think so.'

'Why?' How dare he not want my mother?

'I don't think she'd have me. She wants space and privacy.'

'Oh.' I had expected to feel relieved but I don't. 'Good night then.' I turn to go in.

'You'd better get yourself dry, Emily. I should have taken you to the meeting by car, with you just being out of hospital last week.'

'Oh Roger, don't fuss.' I push my wet hair back from

my face. 'Loosen up. There are worse things than getting wet.' I look up at the drifting rain. I think of how Matchlock craved it, to cool his fever and ease his thirst. Rain and sleet and candleleet . . . He was in delirious extremity and I did not even manage to give him water. That has tortured me ever since.

I go into the house. I don't hear Roger's door open or close and I get the impression that he's just standing there on the pavement getting wet.

Oh well, I decide, if Roger can stand in the rain and be miserable, then so can I. It sounds as if Mum is in the bath. I walk straight through the house and out the back door and stand in the plague-grey alley where water is dripping off the slimy tuffets of moss in the crevices of the opposite wall.

'Seth?' I say out loud. I want him to be safe. I want him not to be a murderer. I want him not to like Alice better than me.

Is it murder to smash someone's head in with a stone if they have tried to kill your cat? Yes, I suppose it still is.

The rain is dripping from my hair, down my face and neck. I am glad to be here, in this century, aren't I? It would be madness to be like Alice and want to go back to the seventeenth century. I'm not as crazy as Alice Smith, am I?

I hum a few bars of 'Greensleeves', then try singing it in my tuneless and inadequate voice.

> *'Alas, my love,*
> *You do me wrong*
> *To cast me off*
> *Discourteously*
> *And I have lovèd*
> *You so long*
> *Rejoicing in your company . . .'*

—— 181 ——

From somewhere up the hill comes the plastic clatter of a dustbin lid. Very twentieth century.

I go in and sit on the Restoration coffer. Pardoner comes and sits with me. Water drips off me and on to the uneven, satiny surface of the wood. Pardoner pats at it with his paw, then licks it up. I stroke him.

'He'll have to manage without you, Pard,' I say. 'You're safe here with me now.'

I can hear Mum singing in the bathroom next to the kitchen. She must have heard me outside because she too is now singing 'Greensleeves'.

I wish Jonah were here instead of over the road at Matthew's. I would quite like to go up and change out of my wet clothes, but along with all the other things I can't be bothered with tonight, I can't be bothered with the emotional stress of getting past Jonah's room, particularly since it now feels even more dangerous empty than it did occupied.

I decide to make myself bacon and eggs.

'Do you want bacon and eggs, Mum?' I shout through the bathroom door. But she has turned the taps back on and cannot hear me.

I put the bacon under the grill and break the eggs into the pan. Time to take my tablets. I feel a slight lifting of spirits at the realisation of how much better I feel. The eggs spit and stutter in the hot fat and I wait for them to go brown and crunchy round the edges.

'Emily,' says a woman's voice.

'Yes?' I have replied before my brain has registered properly that it was not, as I had expected, Mum's voice speaking.

Carefully I move away from the sounds of cooking.

'Yes?' I repeat. Nothing. I move slowly out of the kitchen towards the bathroom. Maybe it really was Mum.

The bathroom door is still shut and Mum has moved on to singing 'Amazing Grace', taking full advantage of the bathroom's echoey acoustics.

Oh well, that's it then. I really am going mad. Fine. Ghostly sounds from the past are one thing, but voices in my head addressing me directly are quite another.

My eggs are burnt. My bacon is on fire. I extinguish the flames and am cramming the lot between two slabs of Mrs Bagling's bread when the smoke alarm goes off. I hate this machine. It sounds like World War Three breaking out and I seem to set if off every time I try to cook anything in the kitchen.

I open the back door to let out the fumes and reach down for the green granite doorstop to prop the door wide until the alarm stops. I wonder how it will feel to hold this doorstop again, after having seen what it did. I hear Mum's voice from the bathroom asking if everything is all right.

'Yes thanks,' I shout. 'Mum, where is the doorstop?'

'Should be in its usual place, just outside the back door.'

I go into the alley and stare all round.

'It's not there, Mum.' For some reason I find that my voice has come out rather wobbly.

'It can't have gone far. Use one of Jonah's boots instead.'

The alarm stops. Slowly, glancing from side to side, I take my sandwich flambé and go and sit down tensely in front of our replacement television. Slowly I relax, as advertisements jabber meaninglessly about cornflakes and cars. Such safe things, I feel as if I love cornflakes and cars simply because they are familiar and friendly and advertisers with jolly voices are being nice to us to persuade us to buy them.

As the adverts end, I glance sideways at the Restoration coffer. I don't know why I do. It just seems to demand my attention. A half hour comedy comes on the television, nothing very funny but also safe, unthreatening. Somehow, though, my attention is drawn back towards the coffer. It stands there, just beyond the corner of my eye, dark and old and beautiful under the window.

Resolutely I stare at the screen and eat my sandwich, taking big dry bites and trying nervously to swallow the chunks before I have chewed them properly. Mum wafts out of the bathroom in clouds of vetiver bath essence and flops down next to me.

'What do you keep in the Restoration coffer, Mum?' I ask, offering her a bite of my sandwich.

She shakes her head. 'No thanks. I don't keep anything in it yet.'

I look over at it again. I find I can't not look at it. I get up and cross over to it and lift the lid, and stop in my tracks. It is full of squat brown bottles and cardboard boxes.

I look over at Mum but she is watching television. I reach in and lift one of the bottles out. A typed label says 'Tetracycline'. I put it back and tip one of the boxes on to its side. 'Streptomycin' says the label. There are tablets here by the hundred, and they look like the missing antibiotic drugs from the hospital. I just stare at them, in astonishment.

'Mum . . .' I look over at the back of her head showing above the back of the sofa. 'Mum, look over here . . .' The head turns, and it is not Mum, but Rachel.

'I am not normally given to petty theft, Emily,' says Rachel after a moment's pause. 'But this was necessary.'

I can't reply. My heart is pounding and I feel rather sick. To my shock, Mum's voice comes from the kitchen.

'Honestly Emily, you've made a terrible mess of this pan.'

I look over towards the kitchen door, struggling for some grip on reality, and when I look back, Rachel has gone. I look into the coffer. It is empty. I turn and run up the stairs, trembling and sobbing. No, no, I want to scream, is there no escape from these hallucinations? Who can help me? Do I need to see a psychiatrist?

A dripping noise is coming from Jonah's room. I fling the door wide and switch the light on. Rain is dripping into the middle of Jonah's floor, on to the bare floorboards. The tarpaulin must have come loose. I move one step into the room and look up to where a corner of the black covering is hanging through the hole in the roof, and there, against the darkness, I see Smiling Reuben looking back at me.

Thirty-one

MY WHOLE BODY CLENCHES IN ON ITSELF LIKE A giant fist, and a tiny grunt of shock comes out of my mouth. Then I start to totter backwards out of the room. I want to scream, but somehow I can't.

They make screaming look so easy in films, don't they. The monster comes round the corner and the heroine just opens her mouth and screams. Now, as I back jerkily out of Jonah's room, all I can produce is a tiny, high 'aah', a whistling, fluting sound, too faint to summon help or to deter this smiling monster.

A dragging noise comes from above. There is the click of tiles shifting. I back through the doorway but my foot catches in a bag of nails left behind by the workmen, and I trip. As I steady myself, the nails scatter all over the floor. I try to drag the door shut behind me but to my horror it jams on the nails.

'Oh no . . .'

There is a creak from above and I see something moving in the hole in the roof. I pull the door with all the strength I possess, holding the edge with both hands. The top bends towards me but the bottom just judders and screeches on the nails. Should I rush downstairs and raise the alarm, possibly endangering Mum if he follows me, or should I try and barricade the doorway of Jonah's room in some way, before he can come through it?

A swooping shadow crosses the light from the wall

lamps in Jonah's room, and there is a loud thud, followed by a snarling groan.

'Devil's work!' hisses the watchman's voice, terrifyingly close. Then, with his voice raised, 'I knew you would try and escape over the rooftops from your pest-ridden house. I knew it. I've been watching for it. They don't call us watchmen for nothing. Hah! You didn't know I had found the hole you made, did you, poor fools!' He laughs and I hear him moving across the room. Then his footsteps stop. 'Now what devilry is this vile brightness?'

Suddenly the door gives. With a squeal the nails gouge the floorboards and the door slams shut. I just get my hands out in time to save them from being crushed. At the same time as the nails squeal, Smiling Reuben screams inside the room and I realise that he has probably touched the electric light bulb in his investigation of the 'vile brightness'. Next moment the handle moves violently in my hands and the door shakes as the enraged watchman tries to open it from inside.

Now, though, the nails are helping me. In the same way that they would not allow the door to shut, now they will not allow it to open.

For how long, though? I rush to my room to find things I can use to barricade the door. Just inside my room is Jonah's chest of drawers. I start to pull it. Roars and bellows of rage are coming from Jonah's room. My breath catches in my throat as I drag the chest of drawers across the uneven landing. Jonah's door rattles on its hinges. Mum's voice calls from downstairs, 'What's all that racket, Emily? Turn your radio down for goodness' sake!' as I push the chest of drawers into place across Jonah's doorway. The watchman is screaming curses now.

Next I must try and move the wardrobe, to barricade

the doorway properly, but how am I going to manage it on my own? I start to edge and lever it along, but it will hardly move.

'Emily?' Mum's raised voice sounds as if it is coming from the kitchen. If she has our old, noisy dishwasher on, she won't be able to hear properly what is going on up here.

'Mum!' I yell. 'Mum, come and help me!'

'Let me help you,' says a soft voice behind me. 'I am strong.'

With a tremor of terror I turn. It is Rachel.

'Rachel! How . . . ?'

'Come, Emily. There is no time. Smiling Reuben is injured, but that has made him like an enraged bull, rather than weakened him. Don't gawp, Emily. Push.'

I push. Together we push and the wardrobe moves. The rattling of the jammed door has become thunderous now, and the growls of fury from inside sound scarcely human. The wardrobe is nearly in position when the door to Jonah's room flies open with a screech.

'Aaaagh!'

He comes out like a wild animal, crashing into the chest of drawers which stands across the doorway, and I see him properly for the first time since he attacked the cat. A new, raw-looking purple scar defaces his left cheek and the side of his neck. He faces us across the chest of drawers that bars his way. Rachel gasps and steps back, but our own way to safety is now barred by the wardrobe.

'*You!*' his gaze flicks over me then comes to rest on Rachel. 'You,' he says more softly, and almost with pleasure. His hand reaches to his belt where I can see a large iron key hanging, and the next moment there is a knife glinting across his palm. 'I had thought you to be thrown into Newgate Prison, murderous beggar, but 'tis well you are here instead. Jail is too good . . .' He fingers the livid scar that now drags his smile down at one corner, then with terrifying speed he pivots over the chest of drawers and lashes out at Rachel with his knife.

I scream then, and Rachel screams too. Our screams reverberate round the narrow landing. We keep screaming — it is as hard to stop as it was to start — and footsteps come running up the stairs. A door slams somewhere, then another. Voices are shouting. I see that blood is dripping from Rachel's hand, then people are pushing the wardrobe from the other side, forcing the watchman to back towards my room. His knife flashes in front of my eyes. He is so close that I can smell his smell of dead leaves and dried blood. I cringe into the corner of the landing and he thrusts his face right at me, smiling lopsidedly, unendingly, his blackened teeth like the chimneys of Hound Hill.

'Emily! Emily!' It is Mum's voice. She forces her way round the wardrobe. I hear Roger shouting at her to get out of the way and let him come through first, but she ignores him. 'What on earth . . . ? Who are these people . . . ? How did . . . ?'

More footsteps come thundering up the staircase but there is no room for anyone else on the landing and I can hear them crowding together on the stairs.

'What's going on?'

'Are you all right?'

'Is somebody hurt?'

It sounds like Jonah and Matthew. The watchman's gaze moves quickly to and fro between Rachel and me and Mum, and the invisible throng behind her. An expression of bewilderment grows on his face.

'Why come you into a plague house, good citizens? I am merely chastising escapers, those who would endanger us all. See what this one did, mistress?' He touches his barely-healed wound with one hand and points his knife at Rachel with the other.

'Did you do that?' demands Mum in a horrified whisper.

Rachel nods. 'Yes. I tried to cut his head off.'

Mum gives a shocked gasp, then instinctively steps towards me as if to drag me to safety.

'It's all right, Mum,' I say shakily, hardly able to take this in. I turn to Rachel. 'You mean ... with that sword ... ?'

Rachel nods, then gazes across the landing as Roger pushes his way to the top of the stairs. There is a shuffling and shifting as Jonah and Matthew reposition themselves and try to see. I hear an exclamation from Roger. At the same moment the watchman pushes me out of the way and vaults back over the chest of drawers into Jonah's room. He crashes the door shut behind him. We hear his footsteps thumping on the bare floorboards, then loud dragging sounds, metal on wood. Almost immediately Roger and Jonah have the door open again, but all there is to see is a workman's ladder poking up through the hole in the roof, and flapping black tarpaulin hanging down.

It sounds as if more people are coming into the house downstairs, attracted by the commotion.

'What's happening?'

'Is anyone hurt?' Voices call up the stairs. I see that Rachel looks very white and shaken. Blood is still dripping between her fingers. Roger and Jonah turn back from Jonah's room.

'I'm going to ring the police,' says Jonah. 'He's gone over the rooftops. He was obviously intending to burgle us. He might be the same one who took the stuff last time.' He edges past Mum and Roger and I hear him reassuring people as he goes downstairs. 'It's all right.

— —

Thank you, but it's all right.'

Rachel is now binding the corner of her bakehouse servant's pinafore round her bleeding hand. With a look of extreme trepidation Mum says, 'Well I don't know the rights and wrongs of it all, but we'd better do something about your hand.'

Roger gives one last look round Jonah's room, then he comes back on to the landing and he too stares at Rachel.

'Where have you been?' he asks in a puzzled voice. 'Everyone has been so worried. And what are you doing here, Alice?'

Thirty-two

*T*HE CROWD DON'T SEEM TO WANT TO GO AWAY. There are still people outside on the pavement when the police arrive.

'Burglars got in through the hole in the roof,' I hear someone telling the police as they step out of their car. 'Armed to the teeth they were. Knives, guns, grenades.'

'Get away, Betty,' says another voice. 'Just a sawn-off shotgun, that's all it was.'

'Well someone got injured . . .'

'They escaped over the roof. It could be our house they do next. Best get home . . .'

Jonah lets the police in and they take statements from all of us. All I can tell them is that I went upstairs and there was a stranger in Jonah's room and because I thought he was going to ransack the house and harm us, after the door accidentally jammed I tried to barricade him in, with the help of Alice Smith who had just arrived.

'Would you be the Alice Smith who's been missing?' demands the policeman. She agrees that she is, and says that she had no idea people would be worried. She has just been visiting friends. The policewoman nods sympathetically.

'Sometimes you do just need to get away,' she agrees. 'I expect what with all the press attention you've had, it must have been a bit overwhelming. We'll cross you off our list.'

At last they go, promising they will keep us informed. Mum shuts the front door firmly.

'I'm going to make some tea,' she announces, and goes into the kitchen. Jonah and I sit on either side of the fire. Jonah prods the flames and adds more coal. Roger sits down facing Alice.

'Well?' he demands.

She stares down at her hand now neatly bandaged.

'I had to go back.'

Roger sits on the edge of the armchair, for once not bothering that one of the cushions has fallen on to the floor. 'Alice, you talk as if you can come and go at will . . . is this really possible?'

She gives a small nod. 'It's a question of wanting to . . . enough.'

'Why? I really don't understand. Surely no one in their right mind would want to go back to the plague year.'

'There was someone . . . *is* someone . . . I have to go back for.'

I look from one to the other of them. So it's true. She is going back to be with Seth. Yet something is puzzling me. Why, if this is so, did Seth not appear to recognise her when she and I arrived at the bakehouse for the first time? Can time be as disordered as this? Or is Seth capable of even greater deception than I had imagined? Alice looks up at Roger.

'Thank you for trying to help me before, Roger. I did appreciate it . . . all our talks about the Beggarsgate phenomenon, and trying to make me see sense. I just can't help it though. I have to go back to comfort someone . . . he has just contracted plague . . . he has the first signs and the examiners of health have shut up his house again, after only just opening it from the previous forty days . . . Can you imagine what that feels

— 193 —

like, to have been imprisoned for forty days watching someone die, then to be imprisoned again for another forty with your own illness?'

'Oh!' My shocked whisper stops her. 'Oh no, is it true? Does Seth have the plague?' I ask her.

'Seth!' Alice frowns at me. 'Who is talking about Seth? Seth is a mere youth. No, Seth does not have the plague, not as far as I know anyway. It is Job I must go back for. Job, who is an honest man with fine feelings and a voice like an angel . . . It is too soon for him yet, but perhaps later when he is over Sarah, he will care about me . . .'

There are tears in her deep-sunken eyes. Her voice still contains the sound of the seventeenth century in it. The tears spill over. 'Job caught the plague after Matchlock broke into the bakery. There must have been plague fleas in his clothing . . .' She clasps her hands together in her lap and her voice drops so that it is barely audible.

'It is my fault. I have loved Job ever since I first went back into the plague year. I worked for the farynor where Job bought his flour. When the plague started in earnest and the farynor fled, I was turned out into the streets. I stayed close by the bakery as much as I could, and when I was given work there I was so happy . . .' She is briefly unable to continue.

We wait, listening to the sounds from the kitchen, and at last Alice resumes speaking. Mum comes and stands in the kitchen doorway and listens. Alice sinks her face into her hands and her voice comes out muffled through her fingers and bandages.

'I can't believe I was so stupid as to open the bakehouse door that night. I thought I was helping Job by serving his first customer after the lockup, and anyway I was too afraid to refuse Smiling Reuben. But because of me, Job now has the plague.'

There is silence. The kettle clicks off in the kitchen. Mum goes to make tea and returns a few moments later with a laden tray.

'Only digestive biscuits, I'm afraid. Oh dear.' She looks at Alice who is now crying openly.

'So after Pardoner ran away, what happened?' I prompt her. She glances at Mum and accepts her tea with a strained smile.

'Seth was going to hit Reuben with the stone. He was beside himself at what had happened to the cat. I don't think he would have killed him, but he didn't get the chance to try, because everything that Reuben had ever done to me while I was begging on the streets, telling the constables and deputies that he had seen me stealing, telling the churchwardens that he had heard me blaspheming and mocking the dead, so that I was thrown into jail for a while then nearly hounded out of the parish, all the persecution and humiliation, suddenly flashed before me and I . . .'

'You were begging on the streets?' Mum interrupts incredulously. The doorbell rings as she is speaking. Jonah goes to answer it.

'I tried to behead him with Seth's sword. I won't compound the wrong by pretending otherwise. Now I am going back to comfort Job, and if I can, to make him well. Then when I have made him well with the drugs I took from the hospital, and when they allow us to open up the bakery again, I shall make as many more people well as I can. Here in the twentieth century you can make more drugs. Where I am going, it is those I stole, then no more for three hundred years.'

'Oh hello, Mrs Bagling,' Jonah is saying. 'Hello. Yes, come in.'

Mum stands up to greet Mrs Bagling. Alice gazes into the fire and adds, 'It's what I have to do to compensate, you see, because I can't stop blaming myself for everything that happened, my stupidity in letting the watchman in in the first place and forgetting to bolt the door again, my clumsiness in accidentally revealing the cat's hiding place, the brief moment when I felt murderous enough to kill Reuben . . . It's all my fault.'

'Hello.' Mrs Bagling comes into the room. 'Someone else to see Emily. He arrived at the front door at the same time as I did.'

We all look beyond her.

'It's actually my fault,' says a voice from the shadows by the front door. 'It's all my fault, not yours, Rachel, and I have been blaming myself for a long time now.'

He is indistinct in the ashen pink light from the low fire. I stand up.

'Seth?'

He holds out his hand to me and Mum gives me a very startled look. I introduce him in a voice that manages to sound surprisingly calm. It is obvious that all of them can see him.

'This is Seth, everyone.'

There are nods and smiles. Seth and Alice exchange a wide-eyed look of astonishment. Mrs Bagling looks like someone on whom horrified realisation is just dawning. I can see she doesn't know what to believe, whether she has finally been caught unawares by the terrors she had refused to face, or whether this is just a very strangely dressed young man. Mum too is staring at Seth's clothes. She suppresses a smirk.

'Where is Pardoner?' asks Seth.

'I put him upstairs when the police came, to make sure he didn't get out,' Jonah replies, gazing at Seth with an expression of fascination. Seth nods approvingly.

'I'd like to see him.'

I hesitate. 'Seth, you can't take him back.'

Mum puts her hands to her mouth. 'Oh no! This isn't Pardoner's owner, is it?'

I nod. 'Yes, Mum.'

Seth shakes his head. 'No, I understand. I am not asking to take him back. I simply want to know that he is safe, and to see him.' He looks at me and comes forward into the firelight. We sit down, me on the arm of Roger's chair and Seth on the antique oak stool next to the fireplace. He speaks quietly in the long-gone intonations of English that I have come to understand.

'I did a terrible wrong in concealing my cat. I know that. It seems even worse for someone who is studying the law, to choose to break it, and it nearly resulted in a watchman being murdered. I could easily have murdered him myself. It also resulted in Pardoner roaming the streets, lost and injured . . .'

He pauses and rubs his hands over his face. 'I . . . I have searched for him ever since. I could not stop myself. I swore that I would find him somehow, no matter how long it took, no matter whether either of us was dead or alive.'

I reflect that it is probably a good thing that most of those present are obviously finding Seth's speech too difficult to understand.

'Do you know the state your cat was in when we found him?' Mum asks him angrily. 'He was starving.'

Seth looks distressed. 'He must have been too badly hurt to feed himself.'

'He was,' she replies, clearly making a guess at the general content of what he has said. 'He must have been wandering for an awfully long time.'

'Yes, he was.' Seth smiles at Mum, and she thaws.

'Come on,' I say. 'Let's go and find the cat.' I stand up, then glance over at Alice as Seth stands up too. 'What happened to Matchlock?' I ask her. 'Will you be able to save him?'

Alice shakes her head. 'No, I wish I could, but it's too late for poor Matchlock. He went mad with the pain of his swellings. You saw how crazed he was, didn't you. A lot of people couldn't bear the pain, or just went mad with the disease anyway, and shot themselves or drowned themselves or threw themselves out of windows or burnt themselves alive. Matchlock was in such torment, and with no one who would come near him to help him, that after he had smashed up the bakery, he went screaming along the alley between the houses and threw himself down the well in the court-yard.'

Roger has gone very white. Mum and Mrs Bagling are staring wordlessly at Alice.

Alice's tone is very bleak when she speaks again. 'So you see why I had to steal the drugs (Mrs Bagling gasps.) and why I have to go back. If I could have stolen antibiotics for injection that would have been even better. In fact I have done, just for Job, because I think he will trust me, but I'm afraid that most people would be too suspicious of syringes and hypodermic needles to accept them. I must go back and just do what I can.'

There is determination in her eyes, an almost fanatical glint, and I feel sure that whatever the difficulties, somehow or other she will achieve what she intends.

I walk slowly towards the stairs, but Alice calls me back. 'Emily?'

I look at her enquiringly.

'I knew from the beginning that you were from the twentieth century. I knew by your clothes. I cannot tell you the shock I felt seeing a girl in Levis in seventeenth century London, that night when Charlie threw a brick through the window of the churchwarden who had turned him out into the street.'

'It was the DSS office.'

Alice smiles. 'Yes well, names may change . . .'

Mrs Bagling tuts reprovingly and Alice throws her a placating smile. 'Anyway, I couldn't say anything to you, Emily, for fear of giving myself away in front of my friends, and after that there was never the opportunity to speak to you on your own.'

I smile back at her.

'I understand. You did make a very convincing beggar, but it must have been terrible, and so dangerous. Are you really sure you want to go back?'

'Oh yes.' There is absolute certainty in her voice. I nod, slightly awestruck, and turn to lead the way upstairs. Seth follows close behind me.

We find Pardoner asleep on my bed. Seth sits down and strokes him. He looks overwhelmed. The little cat purrs in its sleep. I wonder whether Pardoner dreams of rats and plague or of Kit-e-Kat and the jangly ball he chases round the kitchen floor. Perhaps cat-dreams are a mixture of past and present, love and survival, like anyone else's.

'He won't go into Jonah's room,' I tell Seth. I keep my tone neutral so he won't know that I have seen the tears in his eyes.

Seth looks out through the open door, past the jumble of furniture, to where his old room used to be. 'I suppose, even though things have changed so much, he knows the place is the same. A terrible thing resides in Jonah's room, Emily. It is my guilt. Perhaps it will be there for ever. I risked people's lives by hiding my cat.'

'No Seth, you're wrong.' I sit down on the other side of Pardoner and stroke his scarred head with my finger, and my hand touches Seth's, a warm human hand, like mine. 'A terrible thing does reside in Jonah's room, Seth, but your guilt is only in your head. You did what probably lots of other people did. Those were terrible times. It is unreasonable to go on feeling guilty for so long, simply because you protected an animal you loved.'

Seth takes hold of my hand, as he did once before, far off in time but close in space, and for a moment I have an odd flash of gut understanding of the theory that Mr Levin, the physics teacher at my old school, expounded so patiently and repeatedly to our uncomprehending faces, the theory that scientists believe time and space to be the same thing. The time/space continuum is a difficult concept, he would say in an excited, far-away voice, and Rose would say not half and Samantha would look as if it made perfect sense to her.

I smile at Seth and offer a twentieth century tissue for the one seventeenth century tear that escapes his tight-lipped control.

'Pardoner is safe now, Seth. He is happy here with us and we will always look after him and make sure he is well cared for.'

Seth sits silently for a moment. Then he stands up and leans against the wall and fiddles with the ribbons on his sleeves.

'May I come and see him sometimes?' he asks abruptly. 'I have searched for him for so long. Unless you do not wish it, of course . . .' He goes back to the cat and picks it up and cradles it against his cheek, as he did once before. The downy black fur fans out over the tired shadows beneath his eyes. Pardoner stretches in Seth's large hand and purrs loudly.

'It's never stopped you before,' I grin. Seth narrows his eyes and smiles back at me. I am glad to see that humour survives the centuries. 'No really, do come,' I add. 'I hope you will.' I move away to give him time with his cat. Outside my window, the lamp in the courtyard shines on the gold and brown leaves of the oak tree, the tree that grows bent and twisted from the place where Matchlock fell.

I stroll round touching the furniture and thinking how good it will be to have the roof mended and all the furniture back in its proper place. From downstairs I can hear the rise and fall of voices, in cadences of explanation and incredulity.

I go and stand in the doorway of Jonah's room. At once the old fear prickles my spine. I suppose it would have been too much to expect it to go, like magic. Things happened here. They cannot be undone. Somehow we have to find ways of living with them, and go on.

I stoop and start picking up the nails one by one and putting them neatly into the bag. I cannot do anything about the Beggarsgate phenomenon but, like Roger, I can deal with the small things.

Perhaps the past will always be here, on Hound Hill, some of it good and some of it terrifying, all of it creeping, dancing, hopping and weeping across the centuries. The possibility that Smiling Reuben could appear in my room at any moment is part of the price I pay for having seen the past with my own eyes. Seth's friendship is, perhaps, the prize I gain for all the fear and nightmares still to come.

Author's Note

The Great Plague of London in 1665 was the last major outbreak of black death in England. Official figures from the time record that it killed 68,596 Londoners out of an estimated population of 460,000. At the peak of the epidemic, however, so many people were dying uncounted, and sometimes unburied, that the real number of deaths from plague is considered likely to be nearer 100,000.

The following books were of particular use and interest in researching HERE COMES A CANDLE TO LIGHT YOU TO BED:

Albert Camus	The Plague
Daniel Defoe	A Journal of the Plague Year
James Leasor	The Plague and the Fire
Samuel Pepys	Diaries